The Prairie Bride

or,

the Squatter's Triumph

BY MRS. HENRY J. THOMAS,
author of *Border Bessie,*
(Dime Novel No. 146)

With an Introduction by Chris Enss

TWODOT®

GUILFORD, CONNECTICUT
HELENA, MONTANA
AN IMPRINT OF THE GLOBE PEQUOT PRESS

A · T W O D O T® · B O O K

The Prairie Bride; or, The Squatter's Triumph (Dime Novel No. 178) was previously published by Beadle and Company in 1869.

Text by Chris Enss © 2006 Morris Book Publishing, LLC

Text design: Lisa Reneson

Library of Congress Cataloging-in-Publication Data
Thomas, Henry J., Mrs.
  The prairie bride, or, The squatter's triumph / by Mrs. Henry J. Thomas ; with an introduction by Chris Enss.— Rev. ed.
      p. cm.
  "A reprint of the classic Beadle dime novel."
  ISBN-13: 978-0-7627-4083-3
  ISBN-10: 0-7627-4083-3
  1. Women pioneers—Fiction. 2. Frontier and pioneer life—Fiction. 3. Great Plains—Fiction. I. Title: Prairie bride. II. Title: Squatter's triumph. III. Title.
  PS3029.T38P73 2006
  813'.6—dc22
                                        2005037606

Manufactured in the United States of America
Revised Edition/First Printing

AN INTRODUCTION TO
BEADLE & ADAMS
DIME NOVELS

An extraordinary series of books was offered to the public in 1860. The editors at Beadle & Adams Publishing proudly presented reading material specifically geared to the female market. With few exceptions, dime novels authored by women centered on fearless females who braved the open prairie beyond the Mississippi, where they encountered outlaws, warring Indians, and wild animals and endured frigid temperatures, searing heat, and torrential downpours. These fictitious heroines faced desperate challenges bravely, but maintained their beauty and femininity. The combination of determined spirit and classic charm made these characters admirable. They also served as role models for young girls and women—in particular, those hoping to find a better life beyond the Rocky Mountains.

Some historians suggest government officials encouraged dime novel publishers because the books helped persuade settlers to travel to the New Frontier. The country was on the verge of a civil war, and western migration had slowed as a result of the impending conflict between the North and the South. During the war, the Union sought to encourage the continued expansion of the U.S. boundaries and used every means at their disposal to do so.

Politicians recognized women could bring social order to the uncivilized West. The quicker the West was tamed, the easier it would be to claim the territories and their riches to help fund the North's

*Advertisement for the first Beadle & Adams
dime novel as it appeared in the
New York Tribune, June 1860*

cause. Critics who believed that dime novels were being exploited to further the North's cause felt the books were harmful because they promoted an unrealistic idea of life in a rugged new land.

Beadle & Adams's reason for publishing the popular books was mostly financial. Dime novels were the most popular form of literary entertainment from 1860 to 1915. They were fast, exciting reads, and their size made them easy to transport. Women in the East pored over the material while doing their daily chores or on their lunch breaks. Women on their way west read while on the stage or around the campfire. Beadle & Adams novels focused on dramatic struggles and hardships—often of the American pioneer. A strong sense of patriotism or morality was at the heart of each story.

Brothers Erastus and Irwin Beadle and entrepreneur Robert Adams weren't the first to publish such quick adventure novels—they merely issued the material in a continuous series instead of issuing them sporadically, and sold them at a fixed price of ten cents. The novels were printed on the least expensive, lowest-grade paper available. The type was small, no more than two or three columns. The trim size was 6¾ by 4½ inches, and the books were generally 96 to 128 pages long. Each title was issued in a brightly colored wrapper with an illustration depicting the adventurous subject of the book in a dangerous setting.

As dime novels were not considered by the literary world to be on par with other books, the material was primarily relegated to being sold at newsstands and specialty shops. That restriction did not hinder sales, and the Beadle & Adams Publishing formula proved to be extremely profitable. From 1860 to 1872, the company dominated the cheap fiction market. Authors hoping to get their story read by the company's chief editors had to adhere to very specific submission guidelines.

So much is said, and justly, against a considerable number of papers and libraries now on the market, that we beg to repeat the following announcement and long standing instructions to all contributors:

Authors who write for our consideration will bear in mind that–

We prohibit subjects of characters that carry an immoral taint–

We prohibit the repetition of any occurrence which, though true, is yet better untold–

We prohibit what cannot be read with satisfaction by every right-minded person old and young alike–

We require your best work–

We require unquestioned originality–

We require pronounced strength of plot and high dramatic interest in story—

We require grace and precision of narrative and correctness of composition.

Authors must be familiar with characters and places which they introduce and not attempt to write in a field of which they have no intimate knowledge.

Those who fail to reach the standard here indicated cannot write acceptably for our several libraries, or for any of our publications.

The Beadle & Adams Editorial Staff – January 1861

Many talented writers contributed to the Beadle & Adams publications on their way to becoming literary giants. Ned Buntline, Mark Twain, and Louisa May Alcott were a few of the gifted authors who wrote for the publishing house.

With the exception of famous authors such as Charlotte Brontë, Alexandre Dumas, and Buffalo Bill Cody, the dime novel characters were better known than their creators. Hurricane Nell, the Queen of the Saddle; Lasso Bess, the Trapper; and Mountain Kate were daring women that readers couldn't get enough of. Their exploits and challenges were the topic of many fireside conversations.

At a time when job opportunities for women outside the home were limited, Beadle & Adams employed a number of female authors. Ann S. Stephens, Metta Victor, and Mrs. Henry J. Thomas were among the top moneymakers for the company. Not unlike the women they wrote about, these authors represented a pioneering spirit in the field of popular fiction. Their readership went beyond the western Plains into Europe. Ladies in France and England who enjoyed the romantic tales of the American West yearned to embark on the same quests as the women in the books.

Romance books penned by women were among the best-selling dime novels. As such, proposals on that topic were approved over other subject matter. Male writers in tune with the market submitted love stories under female pennames. Popular Beadle & Adams author Albert Aiken used the pseudonym Frances Helen Davenport, and author Frank S. Finn used the nom de plume Eve Lawless.

By 1891 the dime novel had been replaced by more serious types of literature. Educational books and children's stories had risen in popularity. At the turn of the twentieth century, the Beadle & Adams staff made significant changes in the layout and covers of their publications. They also lowered the price of the material to a nickel. Still, they could never recapture the success the bold, soft-bound novels once knew.

Original copies of Beadle & Adams dime novels are rare. According to historians at the California State Historical Library, if the books are found in a complete set of an author's work and in good condition, they could be worth more than $500.

The language used in these historic dime novels is a combination of Victorian-era English and a vocabulary indicative of the time. In an essay in the Yale Review in 1937, historian Merle Curti wrote of the dime novels that these "fragile, rare, and highly fugitive books will be useful . . . to anyone interested in proletarian literature," and that they "must be taken in account particularly by those interested in the democratization of culture . . . in the rise and reinforcement of our traditions and adventure and rugged individualism, in the development of class consciousness, and in the growth of American patriotism and nationalism."

It is with great pleasure we bring this classic series of Beadle & Adams dime novels to a new generation. We're sure you'll find these melodramatic tales both entertaining and inspiring. Although these books were written more than a century ago, their themes of American spirit and determination, of courage and bravery, of heroism and patriotism, and of friendship, love, and honor are timeless.

DIME NOVELIST
MRS. HENRY J. THOMAS

The motion was not altogether unanticipated; and the peddler, by dexterously throwing his arms between those of his antagonist, and seizing his shoulder with a strong grip, partially relieved his throat from the strangling embrace.

—Excerpt from Mrs. Henry J. Thomas's dime novel *The Wrong Man; A Tale of the Early Settlements,* 1862

Mrs. Henry J. Thomas was among the best-selling dime novel authors, penning ten titles for Beadle & Adams, the leading publisher of these popular stories. Although she was one of the company's top money-makers, Mrs. Thomas's background remains largely a mystery. According to historian Albert Johannsen, who wrote *The House of Beadle and Adams and Its Nickel and Dime Novels,* the definitive book on the publisher's authors, "Not a single word of biography has been found on Mrs. Henry J. Thomas." Some historians suggest she contributed additional stories under the name Colin Barker. Others, including Johannsen, speculate that *she* might have been a *he*—that *Mrs.* Henry J. Thomas could possibly have been the pseudonym for *Mr.* Henry J. Thomas. Still other experts believe Mrs. Henry J. Thomas was indeed a woman, but a woman with a shady past. According to these experts, the author submitted her work to Beadle & Adams in an attempt to escape a life of prostitution. To keep her true identity secret from the publishing world, she used a nom de plume.

No matter what the true story, or her true identity, there is no denying that Mrs. Thomas was one of the leading dime novel authors of her day. Her most successful novel, *The Prairie Bride; or, the Squatter's Triumph*, was also her last. Published in 1869, *The Prairie Bride* was reprinted several times and later found a new audience as part of Beadle & Adams's pocket novel series (much smaller versions of the publisher's most well-read books).

Mrs. Thomas's other novels included *Border Bessie, A Romance of the Kanawha; Old Kyle, the Trailer; or, The Renegade of the Delaware; Ben Bramble, the Hunter King of the Kanawha;* and *The Golden Belt; or, The Carib's Pledge.*

CHAPTER ONE

THE PIONEERS

"By jingo! I b'lieve somebody has jumped my claim!"

"There's smoke comin' out of the chimney, that is certain!"

"Yes, and I see a woman—there's somebody living there, sure."

These exclamations all came from the occupants of a large covered wagon, which had been slowly toiling along over the prairie, and had but just attained the summit of a range of bluffs, near the foot of which stood a rude but comfortable-looking log cabin, evidently of recent construction.

A small stream of water, along whose edge grew a line of cottonwood trees and hazel bushes, flowed in a sparkling thread, just beyond the house, and gave a peculiar charm to the spot.

Andrew Hosmar, the first speaker, had, about six months previous to the opening of our story, left his family in Kentucky while he went to Iowa to select a "claim" from the public lands, intending, if the country suited him, to return for his family, and establish himself where he and his four sturdy boys could "have a chance," as he expressed it, "to spread themselves."

The boundless prairie—the rich black soil so deep and mellow, waiting patiently under its waving green mantle, for the plow and the hand of man to call forth its riches—delighted him; and after spending a few weeks in "looking around," he found a section that particularly pleased him, erected a cabin upon it, made a few other improvements, and then, without taking the precaution of pre-empting it, thinking to do so at his leisure, and not expecting to be long absent, he returned to Kentucky for his family. But, alas!

"The best laid plans o' mice an' men
Aft gang aglee."★

Hosmar was detained in Kentucky nearly three months by sickness, and when, after a tedious and wearisome journey of several weeks, he reached his little prairie cabin, it was to discover another person in possession. In western phrase, some sharper had "jumped his claim."

The party in the wagon remained silent for several moments, but, at length, Mrs. Hosmar, a weak, faded-looking woman, with pale-blue eyes and sun-burnt hair, asked, apprehensively:

"What are you a-goin' to do, Hosmar?"

The man did not reply, but with compressed lips and glittering eyes, spoke a sharp "gee-up!" to his tired horses, and started down the side of the bluff. In a few moments more he stopped before the cabin door.

A man, tall, lank, and in his shirt-sleeves, sauntered out upon the steps as the wagon came to a halt, and saluted Hosmar with:

"How de do, stranger? Want to stop?"

"Ruther reckon I *do!* It's been my calculation fur some time, to stop when I got here!" was the curt reply.

"Ah! is that so? Wal, we ain't much in the habit of keepin' strangers. House is *ruther* small fur that; but ef yer a mind to put up

---

★ This saying is adapted from a line in "To a Mouse," by Robert Burns: "The best-laid schemes o' mice an' men / Gang aft a-gley." Modern readers would recognize: "The best-laid plans of mice and men often go awry."

with sich accommodations as we've got, why—"

"I don't want any of *your* accommodations; this cabin belongs to me, and—"

"B'longs to you? Wal, that's cool, I swear!" interrupted the man on the steps. "Got yer papers in yer pocket?" he added, with an attempt at wit.

"Yes, it belongs to *me,*" replied Hosmar, trying to keep his temper under control and speak calmly. "I built this cabin last spring; I'm here with my family to occupy it, and I want to know what right *you* have to be in possession of it?"

"As good a right as I've any occasion fur, my friend; and ef you'll take the trouble to go to the land-office, you kin find out that this piece of land, and what's on it, belongs to a man named Bill H. Larkins—an' that's me!"

"Well, Mr. Larkins, if you expect to cheat me out of this, you'll find yourself a-dealin' with the wrong man; and the sooner you make up your mind to quit, the better it'll be fur you, fur I swear by the stars, that the cabin I hev built fur my own use shall never stand to shelter your cowardly head!" exclaimed Hosmar.

"Don't make no threats, stranger, 'tain't healthy! and I think that a man as is fool enough to take up a piece of land like this and then leave the country without pre-empting it, or gettin' any title to it, expectin' everybody to walk 'round it and keep off till *he* gits ready to come back to it, ain't *quite* sharp enough to prosper in these diggin's, an' had better travel on a spell till he comes to a place whar thar ain't anybody else 'round!"

This speech was delivered with perfect *sangfroid,* as the speaker deposited a huge quid of tobacco in his capacious mouth.

But Hosmar did not give him a chance to enjoy the morsel, for, with the spring of a tiger, he leaped from his wagon and grasped him by the throat.

"Take that! and that! you infernal rascal! I'll thrash the life out of you!"

The vigorous blows that emphasized nearly every word, seemed likely to make his threat good, for the attack had been so sudden and so furious, that Larkins was taken at a disadvantage, and had it not been for his better-half, the squatter would certainly have fared hardly. But she, seeing the helpless condition of her liege lord, came to the rescue with a stout hickory broomstick, and belabored the struggling combatants so vigorously that—although in the blindness of her zeal, or it may be *malice prepense,* she bestowed as many blows on one as upon the other—Hosmar relaxed his hold and retreated to the side of his wagon, while the rescued husband, as soon as he could collect himself, disappeared within the cabin followed by his valiant helpmeet.

In a moment, however, Larkins reappeared, rifle in hand.

"Now, stranger," he exclaimed, "I'll give you jist five minutes to git into yer wagon an' start; an' the quicker you git out of my sight, the better it'll be fur you!"

"Rachel, hand me my gun!" said Hosmar, quietly, without altering his position.

"Oh, Andrew, *do* git into the wagon an' drive on! What's the use of stayin' here to be murdered!" entreated Mrs. Hosmar.

"Yes, uncle Hosmar, *do.* I am sure that the law will restore your claim to you!" said a pleasant voice, and a young girl leaned forward, and placed her hand coaxingly on Mr. Hosmar's shoulder.

"The *law!* Yes, I've *tried* law before now, and 'a burnt child dreads the fire.' I tell you I'll never give up my rights to that sneak there as long as there's life in me."

"Oh, dear! I wish we'd a-stayed whar we was; I jest expect we'll all—"

"Hand me the gun!" interrupted Hosmar, sternly, and with trembling hands his wife obeyed.

"Bill Larkins, don't stand there like a fool to be shot at; come in and shet the door!" called a sharp voice from within the house.

The man was evidently accustomed to obey, for he made an involuntary step backward, then hesitated, and finally, with a

4

suddenness that prevented a steady aim, he raised his rifle and fired.

As soon as he had done so, he sprung backward into the house and closed the door. None too quickly, however, for a bullet from Hosmar's rifle whizzed through the space which his head had occupied but an instant before, and lodged in one of the logs of the cabin.

The shot, however, which Larkins had fired, proved more disastrous than that of his adversary. Hosmar's horses, alarmed at the scuffling and confusion around them, became exceedingly restive, and the shot, fired almost at random, actually pierced an ear of one of them. This so frightened both animals that they could no longer be controlled, and before Mr. Hosmar could reach their heads or get possession of the reins, they had started off upon the full run.

"Hang to the lines!" shouted Hosmar, as the wagon got ahead of him.

"Oh, Lord! we'll all be killed!" shrieked back Mrs. Hosmar; and the children, more alarmed by their mother's unrestrained terror, than by their actual danger, set up a chorus of screams and yells that were discordantly accompanied by the jingle and clatter of the various domestic utensils stowed in the wagon.

On they went for nearly a mile, when there appeared close before them a stretch of silent, glistening water. It seemed to rise mysteriously among the tall prairie-grass, and to the excited imaginations of the terror-stricken party, it appeared to be a vast lake lying in the bosom of the prairie.

Mrs. Hosmar could no longer hold the lines in her nervous hands, and the young girl, who was seated further back in the wagon, sprung forward, and grasping the reins, tried to turn the horses' heads in another direction, but they were utterly unmanageable and kept straight on.

Presently the horses' feet splashed in the water, and the two women involuntarily closed their eyes in expectation of the dreaded plunge; but it did not come, and, recovering their senses somewhat, they saw that the water was not quite up to the wagon-bed, although they had advanced several rods into it.

But, just as their courage began to revive, the wagon suddenly sank, the bed filled, and the occupants found themselves waist-deep in water, while the horses floundered and plunged, and finally settled down, with not much more than their noses above the surface.

The fancied "lake" was the overflowing of a slough ("sloo") or bayou, many of which are to be found in that part of Iowa, and when the horses with the heavily-loaded wagon came to the bed of the slough, they sank into the mud of the bottom, and could not extricate themselves. After a few moments of fear and trembling, the party in the wagon began to recover their scattered senses. The children were fished up from the water and placed upon articles of furniture, and then the two women began to look around them with considerable anxiety.

"Aunt Rachel! I see two men on horseback, over there to the right. I wonder how we can make them see us?" said the young girl already introduced.

"Hollar! Boys, *you* hollar; I hain't a speck of strength left," cried Mrs. Hosmar, eagerly.

The boys "hollared" accordingly, their voices tremulous from excitement and fear. Evidently they were heard, for, in a few moments, the imperiled occupants of the wagon had the satisfaction of seeing the horsemen stop and gaze around them; then the men turned their horses' heads and rode at full gallop toward the wagon.

On they came, splashing their way through the overflow, until they neared the edge of the slough, where matters were explained, and, with hearty good-will, the relieving hand was extended. Squire Boker and his young friend Clark, by dint of much riding to and fro in the water, succeeded in placing all the occupants of the wagon upon dry land, when "the squire" at once rode off to find Mr. Hosmar, while the young Mr. Clark, aided by "Jake," the elder of the boys, succeeded in cutting the horses loose from the wagon, and getting them also safely "ashore."

The condition of the party was forlorn enough. Their clothing was thoroughly wet—it was already past the middle of the afternoon, and the wind which had been blowing steadily all day, now came sweeping across its unobstructed way in a perfect gale. The wide prairie, with its tall grass rising and falling in the wind like billows of the sea, was all around them; not a single habitation was to be seen; there was nothing with which to make a fire; not a tree, bush or rock to afford them shelter from the penetrating blast.

Ere long the squire returned, piloting Mr. Hosmar to the scene of trouble. It was evident that Hosmar had informed his companion of the cause of the runaway, and the state of his affairs, for the squire exclaimed, as he approached the waiting group:

"You mustn't stand here in the cold! My shanty's jist three mile further on, an' I reckon by pilin' on purty well, you kin all ride, an' we'll be thar in less'n no time. You, Clark, ride on ahead, an' tell the old woman that we ar' a-comin', an' it'll be all right when we git thar."

Squire Boker's shanty was a long, low house, built of hewn black-walnut logs, and consisted of two large, square rooms, with an undivided "loft" overhead, and a "shed-kitchen" in the rear. At one end of the principal room was a large fireplace, in which roared an excellent fire, as the travelers entered.

Mrs. Boker, a pleasant-faced woman of about fifty years, and weighing somewhere over two hundred pounds, advanced to welcome them with cordial hospitality. Almost her first remark was addressed to her husband:

"Squire, you keep that fire a-roarin' while I take these women into t'other room and get them some dry things to put on!"

"I'll 'tend to the fire, Jane, but I hope you ain't a-goin' to squeeze them into some of *your* clothes!" and the squire winked with humorous malice.

All laughed, Mrs. Boker among the rest. It removed all embarrassment. The very house seemed impermeated with the squire's geniality and good-humor.

From her abundant stores, Mrs. Boker quickly supplied her female visitors with the needed change of clothes, then she returned to the kitchen to prepare the tea.

"What a dear old soul she is," said Annie, after their hostess had left them, "and these clothes are as white as snow! Do you know, aunt Rachel, I begin to enjoy my adventures amazingly!"

"Oh, dear me, Miss Annie! If you was to ketch your death, or anything was to happen to ye, what would become of us?"

"Nothing will *happen;* don't be discouraged, 'auntie'—and don't say 'Miss Annie' again, for pity's sake!"

"Wal, I'll try not to. I must say it's wonderful how you've stood the journey—ridin' in a big wagon an' campin' out o' nights, an'—"

"Oh, I've enjoyed it! The weather has been delightful! I love autumn better than any other season. I'm a real autumn rose—that's what poor mamma used to call me, you know."

"Yes, you was born in October; I remember the day jest as well as if it was only yesterday! It was *so* sunny, and bright—I remember yer ma said 'twas a good sign. I was a young gal then, a-livin' with yer ma. Law me! It don't seem no time at all when I look back at them times!"

"It seems a long time to me, auntie. I'm in a dreadful hurry to have eighteen hundred and fifty-three come!"

"Of course you are, and it's no wonder; but it'll come round 'fore you know it, 'most. But I hear Mrs. Boker a-stirrin' around a-gittin' supper ready. I reckon I'd better go out and help her a spell. You set here by the stove and rest ye till supper's ready."

The young girl was left alone, and as she sat there, in the plain and ill-fitting garments which she had put on, half musing, half listening to the excited conversation in the adjoining room, she would have provoked the curiosity of any close observer who might have chanced to see her.

Her features were delicate, but strongly marked, and her air refined. The brown, waving hair was glossy and silken, the small hand was white and smooth, but the garments she had laid aside were plain and cheap in material, and "countryfied" in make; there seemed to be an incongruity between the wearer and the worn.

In the course of an hour Mrs. Boker announced supper. In the middle of the "big room" stood a long and ample table, well filled and neatly spread, and, as the party gathered around it, Mrs. Boker exclaimed:

"Now jest sit up and help yerselves; don't be backward. We hain't got any thing very extra, but I've done the best I could on sech short notice. Travelers ginner'ly have purty good appetites, and kin eat a'most anything, when hard pushed."

If her closing remark was intended as an apology, it was not needed, for the fragrant coffee, prairie-chicken stew, fresh fish, warm biscuits, wild honey, sweet butter, rich cream, and other edibles upon the table, might have tempted almost any appetite.

"So you've got another wagon a-comin', hev ye?" said the squire, resuming the conversation, after they had all got seated around the table.

"Yes, my oldest boy, Sam, and a colored man that I've had livin' with me for a year or two, they are comin' with the other wagon. They stopped to get some repairin' done, and to buy up some corn, and flour, and bacon. We come on and expected to be purty well settled by the time they got along, but that infernal rascal has played smart with my calculations, and upset my arrangements completely."

"Wal, we'll upset *him* in the morning; don't grit yer teeth over him any more. We will have him *out* and you *in* before this time to-morrow."

CHAPTER TWO

A "CLAIM FIGHT"

'Twas the morning of a beautiful day in October; the air was soft and filled with a thin haze, through which the beams of the sun fell in mild and pleasing light upon the prairie. A group of men were gathered around the door of Squire Boker's little log-stable, talking in earnest and excited tones.

"I can tell you what it is," said one, "I'm for giving him his full dues. This isn't the first claim he has jumped; he served *me* a little trick once that I haven't forgot yit, and if he don't git his deserts this time, 'twon't be *my* fault!"

"Don't be so savage, Wilson. I think that if we take him over to the Big Muddy and give him a good ducking, and some sound advice, it will answer the purpose."

"You're mistaken in your man then, for he's as stubborn as a mule, and—"

"*I* say, string him up, if he won't agree to quit!" exclaimed another.

"I reckon we kin skeer him out. He's never paid a cent on the land. That stuff about the papers was all a lie; I know him, and he hain't been there more'n a month. He calculated to sell out and try his luck somewhar' else before spring," said another one of the party.

"Wal, boys, come on!" said Squire Boker, emerging from the stable, and leading out his horse all ready for mounting.

"We're ready; got your rifle, squire? Let's see; here's six of us. All right, go ahead!" and the whole party started off upon a gallop across the prairie.

Mrs. Hosmar and Annie had seen the men collect, and stood at one of the front windows to watch them as they started off. They knew, of course, what the object of the expedition was, and Mrs. Hosmar groaned, and "Oh deared," and "wished they had stayed in Kaintucky," over and over again. Annie tried to administer consolation, but without much effect.

"You know, auntie, that it is quite right that uncle should try to get possession of his place. I presume that when Mr. Larkins sees that uncle is not to be trifled with, he will agree to give up, and leave the place quietly; don't you think so, Mrs. Boker?"

"Wal, to tell the truth, I'm powerful uneasy myself. There's been a heap of trouble 'mongst the settlers with these claim-jumpers, and I shouldn't wonder if there'd be a fight. I couldn't git the squire to say what they intended to do, but I wouldn't be anyways surprised ef they'd lynch this feller if they kin git hold of him, and he'll know when he sees 'em comin' what the matter is, and so—"

"You do not mean to say that they will *murder* the man, do you?" exclaimed Annie, in tones of horror.

"Wal, ef he'll give up and clear out, I reckon they'll let him do it; but, ef he's stubborn, there's no knowin' what *will* happen. Men are dretful critters when their temper's up!"

"There'll be somebody killed, I know, and of course it'll be Hosmar; he's allers foremost in every thing!" groaned the unhappy wife.

"Wal, here comes Mr. Clark," said Mrs. Boker, "and I reckon he knows what they *intend* to do. I'll ask him, any way. Mr. Clark, we want you to tell us what these men are going to do."

"They are going to see what can be done with Larkins, regarding Mr. Hosmar's claim," replied Clark.

11

"Do you think there'll be a fight?" persisted Mrs. Boker.

"I can not tell, of course. The man, they say, is a hard case, and his wife is as bad as he is; but they may think 'discretion the better part of valor,' in this case, and give up the place quietly."

"I thought you was a-goin', too, but I'm glad you didn't," responded Mrs. Boker.

"My arm has pained me badly since yesterday, or I *should* have gone," replied Clark, smiling.

"What's the matter with yer arm—rhumatiz?" inquired Mrs. Hosmar, her mind for the moment diverted from her own troubles.

"No, madam; an old hurt that troubles me sometimes," was the smiling answer.

"Why, you see," interposed Mrs. Boker, looking at the young man with a smile of affectionate pride, "he's been to Californy, was there more'n two year, and of all the times! And as he was a-comin' back across the plains with a lot of other men, they got into a fight with some Injins, and he got wounded in the arm; 'tain't much more'n a week sence he took it out of the sling. The whole lot—thar was twenty of 'em—come along here on their way home, and camped out, right in sight of the house. You see they was all of 'em purty well used up, and the dirtiest, shaggiest lookin' set! And they wanted to clean up and make theirselves look more like humans afore they got amongst folks ag'in, so they stopped here a couple of weeks a-recruitin' theirselves. Of course the squire scraped acquaintance with 'em, the first thing, and used ter listen by the hour to their stories 'bout Californy. About the time they got ready to leave, Mr. Clark here was took down with a fever, and the squire persuaded him to stop with us till he got well; so that's the way he come to be here, and I dun know as the squire'll be willin' to hev him go away at all, he's taken sech a notion to him," and, as the good woman concluded, her ample bosom heaved with a sigh that seemed to indicate that she, too, would be loth to have him go.

"I shall always remember my stay here, with pleasure and

gratitude, Mrs. Boker, and, to tell the truth, I do not feel in the least hurry to get away; you *may* be troubled with me all winter. I have not certainly decided yet," said Clark, smiling.

"You don't say so! Wal, I'm glad you've took a notion to stay. It's purty lonesome here in the winter an' you'll be a heap of company fur both of us!" and the broad countenance of the speaker visibly brightened.

Meanwhile the party of men who had espoused Mr. Hosmar's cause, had nearly reached their destination. When they came to the little stream which ran along about twenty rods in front of the house, they dismounted and fastened their horses to the bushes and young cottonwood trees, which grew along its banks; they then proceeded toward the cabin. The door was closed, and the dingy calico curtain was drawn over the little window as if the family was absent. Near by stood a young man, dressed in a rude but rather pretentious hunting costume, and surrounded by three or four large savage-looking dogs. The squire informed Hosmar that the young hunter was a cousin of Mrs. Larkins, and that, in all probability, his being there at that time was not accidental.

The young man was leaning carelessly upon his rifle, and seemed altogether indifferent to the approach of the men. Not so the dogs, however, for they joined in a chorus of low but fierce growls, and seemed only waiting the word of permission or command to attack the advancing party.

"Good-morning, Sharp!" said Squire Boker. "I see you've got yer family round ye as usual. Is Mr. Larkins at home?"

"There don't seem to be anybody 'round," replied Sharp, glancing toward the house.

"Wal, then, we'll just go in and take possession!" said Hosmar.

"You can try it!" said Sharp, coolly.

"I intend to; come on boys!"

The men advanced to the door, and Hosmar laid his hand upon the latch; he found that it resisted all efforts to move it, and that the door was securely fastened upon the inside.

"We must have something to force it open with!" he exclaimed, and two of the men brought from the wood-pile a log of green wood, and with it prepared to burst down the door, or force it from its fastenings.

"Watch fur game when the door gives way!" cried the squire.

"We'll grab him! Give it a dig!"

Four of the men lifted the log, and rushed at the door with a force that nearly sent it from its hinges.

"Hurrah! Another such a lick as that will bring it down!" and the men raised the log for another blow. At this moment the little window near the door was lifted from its place, and Larkins and his wife, each armed with a rifle, showed themselves at the opening. Sharp spoke to his dogs, and they, with exultant yelps, sprung upon the assailants. The dogs were large and powerful animals, and the men were obliged to drop the log, in order to defend themselves.

Snatching their rifles from the place where they had laid them, they tried to beat the creatures off, but it only served to increase their fury.

One of the men standing furthest from the house watched for a favorable chance, and taking a careful aim, fired. One of the dogs rolled over, uttering unearthly howls of agony. Sharp, who had remained standing in apparent unconcern, now seemed to lose all self-control, and rushing upon the man who had fired, struck a blow with the butt of his rifle, which laid the settler senseless on the ground; then, with his gun still clubbed, he sprung into the melée and showered blows on every side.

"Grab the rascal!" shouted Squire Boker, who had received a stinging blow on the side of his face.

Two of the men making a determined rush at their assailant succeeded in throwing him to the ground, and wresting his weapon from his hands; but the dogs, upon seeing their master in need of help, sprung to his defense, with a fury that could not be withstood, and the captors were obliged to release their hold.

"Curse the dogs!" exclaimed Hosmar, as with the strength of a giant he hurled the log of wood and laid one of the brutes prostrate and disabled upon the ground.

"Good for you, Hosmar! Let's make an end of the other, and then of the *folks*!" cried one of the men.

At this moment, Larkins, who had been watching for an opportunity, fired, and Hosmar's right arm dropped suddenly to his side.

"By the Great Jehosaphat, we're a-foolin' 'round here too long! Some of you fellers watch that window while we bang in the door!" cried the man at Hosmar's side.

At this, Larkins snatched the gun which his wife was holding, and fired almost instantly. Just as he did so, young Sharp stepped between him and his aim, and the ball intended for Hosmar entered the back of the young ruffian's head, and he dropped to the earth with a low groan which was his last complaint.

"Oh Lord! What have you done?" screamed Mrs. Larkins. Her husband seemed to be utterly confounded, and unable to speak or move. The men near the door dropped their weapons and ran to the spot where Sharp lay, and while the thoughts of all were centered on the dead, Mrs. Larkins whispered to her husband:

"You're done for now! And the sooner you clear out the better. His folks will foller you to the ends of the earth ef they kin find you out. You allers was an everlastin' fool! Why don't you start? I'll foller when I kin. Climb up inter the loft, and git out of the little back winder on to the shed roof. Here, take your bridle. You kin ketch your horse; I reckon he's a-grazin' on t'other side of the bluff. Why ain't you a-movin'? Them men kin hev that door down in less'n two minutes ef they're a mind to!"

Larkins, by this time recovering his senses, proceeded to follow his wife's directions, while she, as noiselessly as possible, replaced the window at which they had been standing and drew the calico curtain over it. She then ascended the ladder which led up into the loft, and watched until she saw her husband disappear over the bluff which rose but a few rods back of the barn. Descending to the room below, after some little delay, she opened the door, and went out to where young Sharp lay.

"Is he clear dead?" she asked in a low tone.

"Of course he is," answered Hosmar. "A man don't live very long with a bullet in his brain."

"Bring him in and lay him on the bed," she said, "and some one orto go after his folks."

"Where is his murderer? Where's Larkins?" now exclaimed two or three together.

"On the road to the hot place reserved for the devil and his imps," answered one of the men.

"We'd help him to his journey's end mighty sudden if we had him here!" exclaimed Wilson.

"He'll find his way without help," answered Squire Boker. "And ef he's cleared out, so much the better for this neighborhood; don't try to stop him."

A groan from Hosmar, as some one jostled against him, reminded his friends of the mishap which had befallen him.

"Put your arm in a sling, Hosmar," said the squire, "and go home. There's a doctor at the cross-roads—"

"I shan't leave here until the business we come on is settled. I want to know when I ken have possession of these premises."

"If it wasn't for this poor fellow," said the squire, glancing at the body of young Sharp, "we'd help Mrs. Larkins move out this morning; that's what we come for. Thar's nothing like bein' neighborly and givin' yer friends a lift when they need it. As things hev happened, I reckon we'll hev to wait a spell—mebbe she'll set a day, herself?" and the speaker turned toward Mrs. Larkins as if expecting a reply.

"I shan't stay here another night!" she exclaimed. "If some of you will go after his folks, I'll be gittin' things ready so than I kin leave when they do. Tell them to bring a wagon. But why don't some of you carry him in? Oh, Lord, what *will* his mother say?"

The body was lifted from the ground, and taken into the house. They laid it gently and tenderly upon the bed—straightened the helpless limbs, closed the sightless eyes, and then, after deciding that Wilson should be the bearer of the news to Sharp's family, prepared to leave. Mrs. Larkins watched them with a sort of sullen anxiety as they passed out of the room one by one; it was apparent that she dreaded to remain alone with the dead, but her stubborn pride would not permit her to ask any one of them to stay with her. When all were gone she followed them to the door, and watched as they mounted their horses and rode away; then, with a long-drawn sigh, she threw an old shawl over her head, went out of the door, closed it softly and carefully after, and then, with quick steps, mounted to the summit of the bluff to watch for the arrival of her expected relatives.

CHAPTER THREE

THE BURNT CABIN

It was evening. A full moon shed its brilliant light upon the boundless prairie. The wind rustled in the tall, dry grass, and ever and anon the shrill bark of the prairie-wolf could be heard, one voice answering another from point to point, on every side. A bright light shone through the uncurtained windows at Squire Boker's. A large, white-covered wagon stood before the door, and the "big room" within presented a cheerful and comfort-suggesting picture.

The large dining-table stood in the middle of the floor just in front of the fire. Near it, in various attitudes, and engaged with different occupations, were the squire, Mr. Clark, the boys, Mrs. Boker and Annie. One of the group was the boy Sam, who, piloted by Jake, had arrived safely and without mishap, just before dark. Poke, the colored man, and Jake, had gone to the stable to attend to the horses, and see that they were all right for the night.

All had disposed themselves for an evening's enjoyment. What with joke, song, and story it bid fair to be a pleasant evening indeed, when suddenly the door was flung open, and Poke, the negro, burst in, amazement and fear written in every line of his black face.

"Oh, de good Lord, de worl' is afire!" was his loud exclamation.

All sprung to their feet and rushed from the house.

"'Tis the prairie afire!" exclaimed Mr. and Mrs. Boker together.

"Oh, mercy! Is it a-comin' here?" cried Mrs. Hosmar, in great alarm.

"The fire can't cross the slough, an' 'twouldn't hurt us any if it did, for there's nothin' close here to feed it," replied Mrs. Boker.

The fire was in the east, and it rapidly lengthened its line from north to south, and came rushing on—carried by the wind which was blowing into the west—rising and falling, making great leaps, and shooting up in columns of brilliant flame where but a moment before all was darkness.

The whole party stood watching the sublime sight for some time in silence. Then Mr. Clark remarked:

"It seems to me that there is a steady light back there that does not come from the burning of the prairie. It appears to be beyond the present line of fire. Don't you notice it, squire?"

"I b'lieve there *is,* Clark. Yes; I'll bet my three yoke of oxen that that infernal Larkins has sot fire to the cabin and started it in the grass!"

"We was fools fur lettin' him slip away this morning!" said Hosmar, bitterly.

"He'd a-been enjoyin' a fire in another place, if we'd a-served him as we ort to a-done, and as he deserved!" answered Boker.

"Wal, he's played the trump card ag'in' me!" groaned Hosmar, as he turned to go into the house.

"Don't be altogether discouraged, friend!" said the squire, kindly, following Hosmar, and sitting down by the side of the lounge whereon he had laid himself. "If yer cabin is burnt up, there's plenty more timber a-growin' down on Mill Creek bottom; you've got teams and so hev I. 'Twon't take long to build another."

Up to the slough came the broad belt of fire, but no further, and ere bedtime came it had spent its fury and died away in smoke. Only where stood Hosmar's cabin the bright gleam of flame showed that there more fuel than grass had been given up to the destroying element.

The next morning, immediately after an early breakfast, the two oldest boys mounted their horses, and started off to investigate the matter of the fire. They found the grass burned down to the very edge of the slough, and riding rapidly onward, over the blackened sod, they soon came to the smoldering remains of their father's cabin. They returned to Squire Boker's with the information, without loss of time; and then, with Poke to help them, and the squire to show them how to manage, they proceeded to the slough to bring out the foundered wagon.

As soon as it was certain that the cabin was really destroyed, Mrs. Boker and Mrs. Hosmar went to work to carry out the arrangements that had been agreed upon the previous evening. By noon, the room which was to be given up to the Hosmars was emptied and made ready to receive their furniture, and when the other wagon arrived, Mrs. Hosmar, with the advice and assistance of Annie—who seemed to enter into the spirit of the occasion with great enjoyment—soon had their room arranged so as to look quite pleasant and homelike.

CHAPTER FOUR

ANNIE

Stephen Howard was one of the best physicians in the quiet little city of L——, in Kentucky. So agreeable were his manners, so sympathetic and really kind his nature, and so unquestionable his abilities, that very soon after entering upon the practice of his profession, he found himself a fully occupied and much-sought-after physician. When it is added that in his early bachelorhood he inherited a large estate from his father, it will perhaps be thought incredible that he should escape all the "arts and wiles" of fortune and husband-hunting maneuverers, and finally marry a lovely and loving little woman, with whom he lived most happily to the end of his days.

This was the truth, however. But alas! his days were not many. At the early age of thirty-five he was carried to the grave, and his wife and little daughter were left to mourn one of the best of husbands and fathers.

According to the provisions of the will which Dr. Howard left, Mrs. Howard was to have control, under certain restrictions, of the entire property, until Annie, the only child, should arrive at the age of twenty—then one specified half was to be the daughter's; and in case the daughter survived the mother, she was to inherit the whole of it.

The particulars of the will were not generally known, and the still young and attractive widow received many offers of companionship along life's thorny path, from those who, doubtless, were disinterestedly anxious to relieve her of the care and loneliness of her position. Mrs. Howard, however, had loved her husband too well to speedily forget or replace him.

But at length, after seven years of widowhood, she *was* persuaded to marry again—and, as is so often the case, it was impossible to tell what the special inducement was, for the favored man was in many respects inferior to some of those whom she had rejected—at least, *they* thought so.

Annie was twelve years old when her mother became Mrs. Norris. She was a gay little sprite, full of harmless mischief, and the life of the house. Her stepfather would gladly have been friends with her, for he was fond of children, but she—although she called him "papa," and treated him respectfully and kindly—would never allow him to treat her with familiar fondness, but always "stood upon her dignity" with him, in a manner that savored somewhat of willfulness. In truth, she looked upon him as an intruder, who had come between herself and her "dear mamma," to make them less indispensable to each other.

But the shadow was not deep enough to cause much unhappiness in a sphere so bright as hers, and four more years fled swiftly by. Then the angel of death once more entered that pleasant home, to summon from earth that gentle wife and mother.

After his wife's decease, Mr. Norris, with the consent of Annie, and such of her friends as he thought best to advise with, sent for a widowed daughter of his, who, with an only child, a little boy of four or five years, was living in her father's old home.

It was of course necessary that, if the wonted establishment was kept up—and such had been the expressed desire of Mrs. Norris—there should be a matron at the head of the family. Annie was willing to consent to almost any arrangement by which she could remain in the dear old home, and at the same time be exempt from all responsibility and care concerning the household. So Mrs. Plyne was sent for, and in due time arrived, being only too glad to be installed mistress of so beautiful and luxurious a home. Indeed, one could but think, upon making Mrs. Plyne's acquaintance, that she would have been contented in almost any sphere, her face and figure were so plump, her chin so near double, and her smile so ready and good-natured; she certainly enjoyed a chat with the cook in the kitchen, or a confidential communication from Patty, the chambermaid, to a degree that might have brought her authority into disrepute among the servants had she not shown occasionally that she could assert and maintain it, as well as anybody.

She took the most assiduous pains to win the affection and confidence of Annie, partly because she really liked and admired her, and partly, it must be confessed, from motives of policy.

As time wore on, and Miss Annie Howard took her place in society, and became the recipient of the many flattering attentions which rich young ladies are so certain to receive, a change came over the home atmosphere.

Mr. Norris, who always had been kind and indulgent to Annie, now grew intolerant of the company of the young people who were accustomed to frequent the house.

Annie's nature was too independent and self-reliant to bear such restraint and interference very long, without resistance, and at length there were but few days passed without a sharp encounter of words or a clashing of wills between them.

Mrs. Plyne succeeded in occupying neutral ground tolerably well, and bore with remarkable equanimity any attack from either party.

One day, after a most aggravating case of interference, in which Mr. Norris rejected an invitation, almost insultingly, which Annie herself was desirous to accept, she gave expression to her indignation in terms of unmeasured resentment, and ended by declaring that she should no longer remain in a house where she was subjected to such mortifications and annoyances.

"Annie! Annie! Did not your mother request—"

"She did not intend to install you as my jailer, nor suppose that you would make yourself a source of constant unhappiness to me. I am no longer a child, and I will not submit any further to be treated as I have been!"

"Annie! You are using strong language! Do you now know that a young girl, situated as you are—the inheritor of a large fortune—will be followed and flattered, and sought after, by persons whose only motives are mercenary? Your path is full of perils, and it is my *duty*—"

"It is *not* your duty to interfere with my actions in the manner you have done, and it is not *my* duty to submit to it."

"Annie, dear, come with me to my room; *do,* please. I want to talk with you," and Mrs. Plyne laid her arm affectionately and coaxingly around Annie's waist. She complied without a word, and after they had entered the chamber, Mrs. Plyne drew her to a low seat near an open window, and began:

"You think, Annie, that father is very unkind, but *I* know that he does not mean to be. I can explain his conduct, though I fear that I am doing a silly thing; still, affairs have come to such a pass, that *something* must be done. The truth is, that father has a *pet plan,* and he has cherished it and thought upon it, until it has become a monomania with him, and has influenced his conduct much more than he himself is aware of. You have heard us both speak frequently of brother Charlie; he is father's only son, and the best brother in the world; he made his home with me for years. Well, it seems that papa has hoped that *some* day you and Charlie would meet, love, and marry, and of late he has realized how many chances there are that you may find some one else to love before you have seen Charlie at all.

"He has written to brother, over and over again, within the last year or two, urging him to come and make us a visit, but Charlie is perverse, and insinuates, pretty broadly, sometimes, that he thinks both father and I are occupying positions the reverse of independent and dignified, but I believe father really expects to have him here some time this coming winter. So, if he comes, and you *do not* fall in love with each other, the matter will be settled at least. I *know* he will love you, for how could it be otherwise? And, as for *Charlie's* merits, he is good and handsome, and has already acquired considerable distinction as a lawyer, and—"

"And so this delightful scheme is the cause of the persecutions and indignities I have had to endure. I now see through the whole affair. Mrs. Plyne—"

"Dear Annie, *do* not be so indignant. You—"

Just then some one knocked upon the door, and Mrs. Plyne crossed the room to open it. 'Twas the cook, and she put her woolly head into the room and inquired for "Miss Annie."

Annie rose, her face flushed with excitement, and her eyes full of fire, and went out into the hall.

"What is it, Minty?" she asked.

"W'y, Miss Annie, Poke, he's come, an' he wants ter see you mos' uncommon partic'lar 'bout som'thin'—so I tole him I'd run up to yer room—"

Without waiting to hear more, Annie descended to the dining-room, and found Poke already there awaiting her.

She had not seen him before for nearly a year, as he had been living at a place in the country, about twenty miles from town, nearly ever since her mother's death.

"Why, Poke, is this you?" she exclaimed, advancing toward him with a smile. "I am glad to see you; how do you do?"

"Oh, *I's* berry well, Miss Annie! I's powerful glad to see *you* a-lookin' so bright. Why, yer cheeks is as red as roses!" answered the man, with a delighted grin.

"They *feel* red just now, Poke; but, tell me how you are getting along at Mr. Hosmar's—how is auntie?"

"She's berry well, an' sent lots ob love ter you, an' said she'd like mos' powerful well ter see you 'fore she goes ter the new country."

"And so they are really going, are they?"

"Oh yes, missus; an' it's 'bout dat berry t'ing I wanted to ax yer advice. Marsa Hosmar's a-goin' to start 'bout next week, an' he says I'd better go 'long. He will let me drive one ob de wagons, an' help him 'round a spell when we gits dar—he says land is so cheap dat I kin git a farm ob my own, an' be as independent as white folks; an', oh missus! If I thort dat was *so,* an' I could send for Melissy after a w'ile, I'd go, sure an' sartin, ef I had to walk ebery step ob de road!"

"Mr. Hosmar has been out there to look for land, has he not?"

"Yes, missus, he hab—an' he says 'tis de mos' beautifulest place in de worl'."

"And you have determined to go with him, have you, Poke?"

"W'y, I thort I'd come an' see you 'bout it, an' ax yer advice on de subjec', an' if—"

"So you come to consult me, after you have fully made up your mind what to do, do you?" said Annie, laughing.

"W'y no, missus," said Poke, a little confusedly. "I wouldn't a-went, noways, ef you's 'posed to it."

"But I am not; I *want* you to go. Must you return home to-day?"

"No, Miss Annie, I's a-goin' to wait till mornin'; I's got some errands to 'tend to."

"Well, then, be sure to come and see me again; I've got something important to talk with you about; and, do not mention the subject of your going West to Mr. Norris, if you chance to see him."

"Berry well, Miss Annie. I'll 'quire for you jest after breakfas' in de mornin'."

"I will be here or in the garden; don't forget."

"'Deed I won't, missus—me mem'ry's perfec'ly reliable in dis case!" and the faithful freedman went his way, looking very wise and self-important.

An idea entered Annie's brain when Poke spoke of going West: she too would go! She was excited and indignant—too much so to

26

consider the subject calmly and in all its bearings; she only thought that she could thus get away from the hateful interference and scheming of her stepfather during the year that must still intervene before she would be entire mistress of herself. As soon as Poke left her, she hurried to her own room to think over and perfect her plan.

Her resentment toward her stepfather was so strong, that she was quite willing that he should endure all the perplexity and disquietude which such a step on her part would cause him; but she did not wish her absence or disappearance to be a subject of wonder or scandal among her acquaintances, and so, after thinking the matter over for several hours, she at length determined to write two or three notes to be sent to some of her intimate friends, as soon as she should be safely out of the way. She wished to word them so vaguely as to give no clue to her real whereabouts, and 'twas only after half a dozen trials that she succeeded in inditing one that she thought would answer her purpose. The following is a copy of one of them; the others differed but little, except in the address:

DEAR MATTIE—I have—quite unexpectedly—an opportunity of going abroad for a few months—possibly for a year—with some old friends. Do not be altogether stunned by this sudden announcement, and above all, do not quite forget me during my absence. Please make my adieux to all "inquiring friends," and believe me, your affectionate friend,

ANNIE HOWARD.

To her stepfather she wrote:

MR. NORRIS—Some friends of mine—old friends of my mother's too—are going abroad; and for reasons which you will doubtless understand, I have determined, without consulting you, to accompany them. It will be too late when you receive this for you to *prevent my going. I shall not return, probably, for a year, when I shall be entirely free to live with whom and where I choose.*

A.H.

"I ought not to have used the word 'abroad,' I believe; it seems to imply that I am going to leave the 'land of the free and the home of the brave'; but what other word *can* I employ that will be indefinite enough?"

Thus mused Annie as she sat at her writing-desk, folding and directing her notes. While she was still puzzling her head about the propriety of using the word as she had done, a servant came up to announce a young lady visitor. Annie ran down to the parlor, and found an old school friend, who lived several miles in the country, and who was then in town to do some visiting and shopping. She had come to urge Annie to accompany her home and spend a few days at the farm. Mr. Norris did not think it wise to object, and the invitation was joyfully accepted.

"Come up to my room, Susie, and lay off your things. Of course you will stop with me during the remainder of your stay in town," and the two girls ran up-stairs to prepare for tea.

That evening, after the girls had retired to their room for the night, Annie told her friend, confidentially, how unpleasant and unbearable Mr. Norris' conduct toward herself had become, and of the determination she had of going West.

Susie Malor, a sensible and kind-hearted girl, feared that Annie might encounter troubles and privations that she little expected; or, worse still, cause gossip and 'wonderment' by such a step, which would be a source of annoyance and regret in the future. Hence she tried to dissuade her friend from the undertaking, but when she found that she could not, she lent a sympathizing ear to every particular of the proposed plan, and promised to aid her as far as she could, in carrying it into execution.

"You can now understand how much your invitation to visit you at this time will help me along. I can pack my trunk with the things I wish to take with me, and no one will suspect that it is for a more lengthy journey than to your house. I will arrange with Poke to come there for me, when Mr. Hosmar is ready to start; and thus, you see, I shall be fairly on my way, while my affectionate friends here at home are imagining me at the farm."

"But, Annie, the Hosmars will of course go in big wagons, loaded down with every manner of stuff—such people always do— and I'm afraid that a young lady of your stylish appearance, traveling in such a way, and in such company, may attract more attention than you will like!"

"I had not thought of that, Sue. I must make a traveling dress. Let me see: a dark delaine dress, made just as Aunt Rachel makes *her* dresses, and a large gingham or calico sunbonnet; a warm blanket shawl, in red and blue plaids, and some thick cotton gloves—won't that be about the thing?" said Annie, laughing.

"I suppose so; but oh, Annie, how wild your plan is!"

"Why, Susie, I shall enjoy it far more than I should a trip to Europe! Just think how free I shall be! And, Susie dear, don't borrow trouble on my account; I will write to you as often as I can, and keep you informed of all my adventures and mishaps, if I have any. I will purchase my equipment to-morrow before we leave town. I shall see Poke in the morning and take him into my confidence; he can make the necessary arrangements with Mr. Hosmar, I will send an explanatory message to Aunt Rachel, and thus you see, every thing will be nicely settled."

"But, Annie, suppose that the Hosmars should object? They may not be willing to incur the responsibility of running away with an heiress."

"I am quite certain that they will *not*. You know that Mrs. Hosmar lived with mamma many years, both before and after her marriage. I have called her 'auntie' ever since I learned to talk. She lived with us until I was nearly four years old, then she married; but mamma always took an interest in her, and I have spent many happy summer months in her care upon the farm, while a child. She loves me dearly for mamma's sake, and she does *not* like Mr. Norris, so I am certain she will not object to encounter any responsibility that I may ask of her."

"You must have money, Annie."

"Of course, Sue. Fortunately, I have four or five hundred dollars on hand, which will meet my 'traveling expenses' and pay my board for a year, will it not?"

CHAPTER FIVE

THE PRAIRIE FIRE

The autumn proved a long and pleasant one. Winter delayed to make its appearance until near the beginning of January. Mr. Hosmar, accepting of Squire Boker's advice, had selected a half-section of land which joined the squire's possessions, and the work of building a new house had gone bravely on.

It was not to be a simple cabin, as the first one had been. Annie had insisted upon paying Mr. Hosmar for a year's board in advance, that he might be the better able to build a more roomy dwelling, for, although he had horses and wagons and farming utensils, his stock of money was but limited, and the greater part of it was intended to buy cattle with, and to meet the expenses of living until a crop could be raised from his new land. Poke being by trade an excellent carpenter, proved invaluable in this emergency. The new house was of course built of logs—it was a story and a half high, with two rooms below and two above. The two upper rooms were divided by a little hall, and one of them was to be finished off in the best manner possible under the circumstances, and be devoted especially to Annie's occupation.

One day, about the middle of December, Mrs. Hosmar and Annie concluded to walk over to the new house, and see how it was coming on. A well-broken path already had been made between the two places, for there was a continual coming and going.

As they approached the house, Annie stopped to admire the scene. The prairie was gently rolling, and the building stood upon a slight rise of ground; behind it, to the east, rose a range of wooded bluffs, while in the west was to be seen the windings of Saw-Mill creek, with noble walnut and cottonwood trees bordering its course. The tall grass near the house had been cut down, and a few furrows plowed around the cleared space, to prevent all danger from fire, should the prairie burn over during the fall. The sound of hammers and saws, busily plied, reached their ears where they stood, and as they moved on again, Mrs. Hosmar remarked:

" 'Twon't be more'n a week or so, I reckon, before we kin move. I shall be dretful glad, fur I feel as if we was a-crowdin' Squire Boker's folks out of house and home."

"I shall be glad, too, auntie, and I am delighted that you are going to have such a pleasant and comfortable home. If Mr. Hosmar has no further ill-luck you will be rich and independent one of these days."

"Mebbe we will, Annie, but I'm afeered *you'll* be dretful lonesome after we get moved over here."

Annie blushed faintly, as she saw Mrs. Hosmar's pale blue eyes fixed with a sort of troubled inquiry upon her face, but replied, laughingly:

"I certainly did not expect to find much society here on the prairie, and perhaps a few months of seclusion and reflection will be good for me."

"Mr. Clark has been a heap of company fur you; but—law me! There he is now."

Mr. Clark appeared in the doorway, and extended his hand to assist Mrs. Hosmar and Annie to climb up, as no step had yet been made before the entrance.

"Mr. Hosmar has just been telling me," said he gayly, "that he intends to have a 'house-warming' on Christmas-eve. *I* am already invited, and have promised to furnish a pair of wild turkeys and some fresh venison for the occasion."

"Do you really s'pose the house'll be done by that time, Andrew?" asked Mrs. Hosmar.

"If the weather stays favorable it will; and I've been thinking that, as we ort to hev a spree, it'll do fur a Christmas celebration an' a house-warmin' both."

"Miss Annie, would yer please to come up here? I wants to 'sult you 'bout some of dese fixin's," called Poke's voice from above.

Annie ran up the stairs, and found Poke apparently in a very undecided state of mind concerning some shelves he was putting up in one corner of the room.

"You see, missus, if dis lower shelf was 'lowed to come out 'bout *so,* a little furder dan de others, w'y den you could use it fur a table to write yer letters on, and fur yer sewin' and trinkets or sich likes ter lay on. W'at does yer t'ink 'bout it, Miss Annie?"

"It would be very convenient for many uses, Poke. How nicely you have finished off these black-walnut shelves; they are quite handsome. And how pleasant this room is; this south window makes it so cheerful."

"I's mighty glad you t'inks so, Miss Annie. We 'spects to git moved over here, purty soon, an' I's mos' powerful glad of *dat,* too."

"Why, Poke, you and Squire Boker are good friends, are you not?"

"Yes, missus, we am; and I hopes you'll forgive me if I takes de liberty to speak on a subjic' dat I knows I's no business to 'fringe upon; but, den, what would Miss Mary say ef I was to see her chile a-runnin' into danger, an' never do nothin' to 'vent it."

"Why, Poke, you are so solemn that you frighten me. What can be the matter?"

"Now, Miss Annie, you mustn't be 'fended, but 'member I've knowed ye ever since ye was borned, and yer mamma, too, and she trusted a heap in my judgment 'bout t'ings."

"Yes, Poke, I know she did."

"Well den, Miss Annie, I kin see dat Massa Clark is a-fallin' in lub wid you mos' drefful bad. Course he can't help *dat,* but w'at I wants to do 'bout it is ter put ye on yer guard. 'Twouldn't do, noways, fer a young lady ob *your* standin' an' 'spectations to encouredge an ordinary person like Massa Clark."

"Poke, I am astonished at you for presuming to speak as you have done. You have no reason to think that Mr. Clark cares any more for me than he does for Mrs. Boker or Aunt Rachel, and if he did, I am certainly competent to judge for myself in such a matter."

"Dar, Miss Annie, I knowed you'd be 'fended; but I've been a-t'inkin' an' t'inkin', as I was a-workin' here by myself, dat maybe 'cause dar's no odder young folks 'round, an' he's so mighty peart to talk and make hisself agreeable, dat yer might—jest from bein' lonesome like."

"Well, Poke, never speak or think of such a thing again. Arrange the shelves in the way you mentioned; you can always contrive to have things just right, so I won't pretend to advise you. I must go now."

But the step with which she left the room was not a very elastic one, and her thoughts, as she went slowly down the stairs, were about as follows: "What put such ideas into Poke's brain, and what did Aunt Rachel mean this afternoon when she looked so sharply at me, when speaking of Mr. Clark? Can it be possible that they so misunderstand me as to imagine that I am going to 'fall in love' with him? How ridiculous," and a scornful smile settled about her lips and lingered there as she entered the room below. No one was there but Mrs. Hosmar, though she could hear Mr. Hosmar and Mr. Clark, talking in the next room.

"Are you going home soon, Aunt Rachel?" she asked.

"Wal, I *did* intend to clear the litter out of this room, an' start a fire in the fire-place ter see ef the chimbly'll draw; but, if you're tired, or in a hurry to go back, I'll go now."

"Oh, no; you can stay until Mr. Hosmar is ready to return if you have any thing to do. I will walk on alone."

"Ain't you afraid to go by yourself, Annie?"

No, indeed; there is a good path, so that I can not lose my way, and it is not very far."

"Bettern'n a mile, I reckon; but, if yer really not a bit afraid, I guess I'll stay a spell longer, and clear out some of this trash."

So Annie started upon her homeward walk alone, and Mrs. Hosmar began to collect the chips and fragments of wood that strewed the floor, and arrange them upon the hearth for the purpose of making a fire.

When all was ready, she exclaimed:

"Wal, now, ef I ain't smart! I wrapped up them matches an' put 'em in Annie's pocket, cause I hadn't none in this dress, an' now I've let her go off without takin' 'em out; but, mebbe Poke's got some—he smokes a pipe."

Fortunately Poke was well supplied with the desired article, and before many minutes there was a roaring blaze in the big fire-place, and Mrs. Hosmar had the satisfaction to find that the chimney "drawed" perfectly.

Presently Hosmar and Clark entered from the adjoining room, and Hosmar exclaimed:

"Got a fire started hev you, Rachel? The chimbly seems to do first rate, don't it?"

"Why, yes, I don't b'lieve it's a-goin' to smoke any; I do 'bominate a smokin' chimbly."

"I wonder who don't? I reckon we'd better go home now. Tell Poke to make the fire safe before he leaves. Whar's Annie?"

Before Mrs. Hosmar could reply, Clark, who was standing in the door, exclaimed:

"The prairie is on fire over yonder. It is fortunate that you have prepared for it, or, with all these boards and chips and other stuff lying under the house and around it, you might have had quite a different 'house-warming' from the one you invited me to a little while ago."

"I noticed that the air seemed smoky, but never thought about the prairie's bein' on fire. I was calculatin' on a spell of Indian summer," said Hosmar.

Mrs. Hosmar ran to the door and looked out.

"Why, it's right between us and Squire Boker's, ain't it!" she exclaimed.

"Yes, Rachel, but you needn't be oneasy; 'twon't hurt any of us. Why, woman, you look as if you was a-goin' to faint."

"Annie, Annie!" she exclaimed, almost frantically, motioning with both hands toward the fire.

"What do you mean, Rachel? Isn't she here?" asked Hosmar, apprehensively, and Mr. Clark turned quickly to catch her reply.

"No, no! She started to go home nearly half an hour ago!"

"Perhaps she has had time to reach the plowed fields by the house!" suggested Hosmar.

"She is sech a slow walker, I don't b'lieve she'd be any whar's near home!" replied his wife, despairingly.

"What can we do?" asked Hosmar, turning to Mr. Clark.

"Nothing!" was the reply. "The fire will pass by us in less than ten minutes, and then I will hasten over to the squire's and see if she is not safely at home."

He spoke calmly, but his lips were compressed and pale, and his gaze was fastened upon the line of surging flame as if striving to pierce the wall of fire and smoke, and tell what might be beyond its savage roar.

Poke had come down-stairs, and stood staring at each one alternately, rolling his eyes in a sort of stupefied bewilderment.

"Oh, Lord! What made us ever bring that child out to this dreadful country!" cried Mrs. Hosmar, bursting into a sort of hysterical weeping.

"Hush, Rachel; we will soon find out where she is, an' like as not she's safe an' sound as we are!"

In ten or fifteen minutes from the time they discovered the fire, it had reached the line of plowed ground which surrounded the house, and Mr. Clark exclaimed:

"I will hasten over to the squire's. The sod is still burning and the ground is hot. You had better wait a little while before you attempt it."

"I's a-goin' too!" muttered Poke. "I reckon I kin afford to spile *one* pa'r o' boots, a-lookin' after my own missus!"

"If Miss Annie is not safely at home *now*, we can neither of us be of any service to her. The fire was terrible, but, come on!"

Swiftly they passed down the path, each one glancing around from side to side, searching for an object that *might* be there; but no, on and on, and still nothing to be seen but the black and smoking prairie. As they neared Squire Boker's, Poke remarked:

"I 'spect I's split dese boots for nuffin'; but Miss Annie wouldn't objeck to 'placin' 'em with a new pa'r, if she had de least supposition ob de 'casion ob de damage."

The squire stood before his door watching the approach of the two men, and as they came up, he exclaimed:

"Why, you fellows must be perfect salamanders. What in thunderation brought you over the prairie jist *now*?"

"Is Miss Annie at home?" asked Clark.

"Why no; she went over to t'other house with Mrs. Hosmar quite a spell ago."

"Yes, yes! But has not she returned?"

"Not as I know of. Why, you look as pale as ef you was scart. What's the matter, man?"

"She started to return home alone, not long before we discovered the prairie to be on fire. We thought she might have had time to reach here before the fire came up," explained Clark, hurriedly.

"The deuce!" exclaimed the squire. "I'll ask Jane, but I don't b'lieve she's here."

No, she was *not* there!

For a few moments is seemed as if a dead weight had suddenly fallen upon every heart; scarcely a word was spoken. Mrs. Boker came out upon the door-step, and stood gazing around her in a sort of bewildered consternation, while Poke threw himself prone upon the ground, and gave way to his grief in a series of groans and ejaculations that were pitiful to hear.

"Oh, mighty Lord!" he murmured to himself. "De las' words I said to dat poor chile, was words dat 'fended her!"

At length, however, the squire spoke. "Clark, we'll git onto our horses and range over the prairie as fur as she could possibly have got to, until we find some trace of her; mebbe she'll turn up safe an' sound somewhar, tho' I'll be dogged ef I kin see how she *could* git out of *that* scrape!"

"We must send word to Hosmar," said Clark. "Here Poke, get up! We are going to search for Miss Annie. You must take a horse, and ride over to the new house; tell Mr. Hosmar that we did not find his niece here, and that we are searching for her. Give him the horse so that he can help us; now hurry!"

It would seem, that with the tall grass all burnt off from the ground, any object upon the prairie, as large as a human being, would be readily discovered, if within a distance of two or three miles; but there are inequalities of surface; hollows and mound-like hillocks, and little ravines which impede the view; and so the two horsemen prepared for a close search, each one taking a separate course across the blackened sod.

Squire Boker turned his horse's head toward the south; he was well acquainted with almost every acre of land that lay within a circle of half a dozen miles of his own farm, and in the course of an hour had satisfied himself that further search in that direction was useless. He had just made up his mind to leave his "beat," and ride over and join Clark, when he discovered a figure moving slowly across the prairie, within half a mile of his own house.

"I'm willin' to swear that's her!" he exclaimed, and standing up in his stirrups he uttered a shout that astonished his horse, and came near being the cause of an unpremeditated descent to the ground on his own part; but, after sitting in dignified surprise for half a moment upon the animal's hind-quarters, he regained his saddle, and dashed off at full speed toward the newly discovered object.

It was indeed Annie; but what a sight! Her face and hands were blackened by the smoke and flying cinders; her dress was scorched and shriveled and torn; she was bonnetless, and her hair was hanging loosely around her shoulders.

The squire called to her to stop, as soon as he approached sufficiently near to make her hear his voice, and as she turned and recognized him, she sunk almost helpless to the ground.

"This is too bad, I vow!" exclaimed the squire, half crying and half laughing with conflicting emotions, as he jumped from his saddle, and bent over the nearly fainting girl. "I ort to of brung camfire bottle along."

"Water—a drink!" murmured Annie, imploringly.

"Thar ain't a drop nearer than home, but we'll be thar in less than no time ef you've got strength to set up. I'll put you on to Nance, an' then git on myself. I kin carry you before me easy, an' then 'twon't take more'n five minutes to git home!"

When the squire was seen approaching the house with Annie before him on the horse, there was a sudden breaking forth of sobs, and cries, and tears, which had been partially suppressed during the suspense of uncertainty.

Mrs. Boker, with many "Oh dear's," and other ejaculations of pity, helped Annie into the house, and seated her in the big armed rocking-chair; and when the water came and Annie had drank, she took a soft, clean towel, and bathed the almost blistered face and hands, and brushed out the long, brown locks of hair, and tucked them neatly up, before she would allow her charge to speak a word.

Mrs. Hosmar made several feeble attempts to be of assistance in some way, and laughed one moment and cried the next, until Mrs. Boker, with kindly authority, bade her sit down and keep still, till she got over her hysterics.

The squire, throwing himself into a chair opposite Annie, exclaimed: "Wal, young lady, you've give us all a considerable skeer! I hain't had sech a palpitation of the heart before, since I 'popped the question' to Jane here, purty near thirty years ago, as I had when Clark came a-rushin' through the smoke and said you was a-missin'!"

"Now, squire, I don't see how you kin talk so silly, when—"

"If I didn't *talk* silly, I'd hev to *act* silly, an' that would be a heap worse. Now, ef you'd any ruther see me in a fit of hysterics, bring in yer camfire bottle! I must let off a little of this excitement some way!"

"I'm very sorry to have been the cause of putting your nerves into such a condition!" said Annie, laughing, in spite of herself, at the idea of seeing the squire in hysterics.

"You'll feel worse when you see Mr. Clark; his hair was turning white at an awful rate when we parted company!"

"Now, squire, you've got to hush up! We're anxious to hear Annie tell how she happened to escape, without gittin' burnt more'n she did," interposed Mrs. Boker.

"Yes, tell us what you *did* with yerself. We hadn't much expectation of finding you alive and well, I kin tell you!" said Squire Boker.

"I haven't much to tell, and it all seems like a strange, wild dream to me! Boys, please bring me another glass of water; my throat still seems filled with the hot smoke that nearly strangled me. When I discovered the prairie to be on fire," she continued, "I was not much more than half-way home. My first impulse was to turn back and attempt to run away from the fire, but in a few moments I found that it was much the swifter of the two, and I soon felt its hot breath sweeping over me. The wind was bringing the flames along with such rapidity, that I quickly saw that my desperate flight would avail me nothing; my bonnet fell off as I ran, but fortunately I had on my woolen shawl, and this I pulled up over my head and face to protect me as much as possible from the heat. The hot wind nearly suffocated me, and my lungs and throat seemed filled with the stinging smoke. Thoughts flew through my brain with lightning-like rapidity; I remembered hearing Mr. Boker relate an adventure of his own, in which he being nearly overtaken by a prairie-fire, would have probably lost his life, had he not succeeded in getting another fire started, and a space burnt over, upon which he remained unhurt while the flames passed on around him. Then, suddenly, it flashed into my mind that there were matches in my pocket, and I might perhaps succeed in saving *myself* in the same way.

"You know, auntie, that you gave me a package of matches when we started over to the new house together—you said that you had no pocket in your dress, and you thought you might lose them on the way. I suppose that your forgetting to ask me for them before I left you, was providential, at least it was a very fortunate thing for me. The instant I remembered the matches, I took them out of my pocket, exerting myself to run still faster for a little way, then I stopped and lighted a bunch and threw them upon the grass; it was so dry that it took fire at once, and in an instant I was entirely surrounded and almost overwhelmed by fire and smoke and an air so hot that I was obliged to hold my breath and cover up my entire face in the folds of my woolen shawl. I followed immediately in the track of *my* fire; my dress was a heavy merino, and my shoes tolerably thick, or my clothing would doubtless have taken fire, but the heat and the exertion overcame me in a few moments, and I sunk to the ground. I must have remained in a sort of stupor for a little while, and when I regained my consciousness and rose to my feet, I was so bewildered, the appearance of the country was so changed, my head was so dizzy, and the sense of danger still so strong, that I could not tell in which direction I ought to go; but I started on, walking as rapidly as I could, scarcely knowing or thinking where I was going, when I seemed to suddenly lose my footing and sink—sink—sink into some unfathomable depth. I do not know how long It was before I 'reached bottom,' but the first thing I was next aware of was, that I was lying in an excavation of the earth, about a foot in depth, and six or eight feet long, and that I must have 'bumped my head' sadly when I fell, for it felt very sore upon one side. I lay still for a little while and indulged in a real good cry, then crept out, and, seeing the house in the distance before me, started toward it, feeling forlorn enough. But I had only walked a little way when I heard a most welcome voice commanding me to 'stop and wait.' It was Mr. Boker's, and now I can hardly realize that my 'troubles are all o'er,' and that I am safely at home."

Annie, having retired to her own little nook, with the assistance of "aunt Rachel," was soon bathed and freshly dressed, anointed with cream, and tucked into bed, where, in a very few moments, she fell into a deep, refreshing slumber.

Mrs. Hosmar then softly left her, and proceeded to the outer room, where she encountered Mr. Clark. He looked tired and pale, and if his hair was not turned white, as Squire Boker affirmed, there seemed to be an additional furrow or two upon his forehead. Upon seeing Mrs. Hosmar, he glanced inquiringly around, as though expecting to see some one else also; and she, interpreting the glance in her own way, answered it, by remarking:

"She's a-layin' down; she was so overcome and tired out that we persuaded her to go to bed an' git rested till suppertime."

"Then she had escaped serious injury?" questioned he, while his countenance cleared up and looked several degrees brighter.

"Wal, she complains some of her throat, an' her face an' hands are purty near blistered; but, I reckon ef we nuss her up for a few days, she'll be 'bout as well as ever."

Mr. Clark seated himself by the fire, and seemed to fall into a reverie.

CHAPTER SIX

HOUSE-WARMING

It was Monday, the twenty-third of December. Winter had at last come in full force. All the day and night before, snow had fallen steadily, and the prairie lay a vast, unbroken field of glistening snow. The sun shone now, however, clear and bright; the sky was blue and cloudless, but the cold was most intense. Roaring fires blazed up the wide chimneys at Squire Boker's. Around the hearth in the "big room" was gathered a group of earnest talkers, composed of all the older members of the two families, while the boys and their prime friend, Poke, held possession of the kitchen.

"I tell you what 'tis, old lady," said Squire Boker, addressing his wife. "I don't b'lieve I kin stand it to go over to Blufftown to-day. If Molly's thar, I reckon she'll keep—it's cold enough."

"Wal, but Jerry was to leave her at the tavern till you come for her, and she'll be *awfully* put out, ef she hez to stay thar 'mongst strangers, over Christmas. Besides, it's been about three months sence she went away, and I want to see her."

"There's a heap of things we ort ot hev before Christmas," said Mrs. Hosmar, "an' it'll take us all day to-morrow to git moved, and ready fur the house-warmin'. Ef Hosmar hadn't invited the folks, I'd be fur puttin' it off till this cold spell is over."

"I reckon 'tisn't so cold as we imagine," said Mr. Hosmar. "We've had such a long, pleasant fall, that we feel this weather more'n we will after we git used to it."

"Wal, when a feller's whiskers git stiff an' white with frost goin' from the house to the stable, it's a sign that it's middlin' cold," replied the squire, shrugging his shoulders and holding his hands over the blaze, as though the very remembrance of the keen air out of doors made him shiver.

"Oh, it's cold, I'm well aware of *that,* but I reckon I'll hev to go to town, anyhow. We're 'bout out of flour, and Rachel wants some fixin's for her Christmas dinner, an' Annie is expectin' letters; so, if you don't want to venture out, I kin bring yer daughter; there's no need of your goin' on *that* account."

"You don't understand this prairie as well as I do; it's middlin' easy to lose your bearin's, jist after a snow-storm, when thar ain't a sign of a road, nor a track of man or beast to be seen! So, ef the old lady's bound to hev Molly home, an' Mrs. Hosmar can't git along without the fixin's, an' Miss Annie is expectin' a love-letter—why, I reckon we'll hev to go!"

"It's only fifteen mile, an' ef you start right off, you can git thar before dinner-time," said Mrs. Boker. "I'll hev some stones heated to put into the sled to keep your feet warm, an' you kin take both buffaloes, or a couple of big blankets for Mary to wrap up in."

"If you are really going," said Annie, "I will make out a list of articles I wish to send for."

"I reckon we'll go; I don't see any gittin' out of it. Rachel, you'd better git Annie to set down the things *you* want, or mebbe I'll forgit something."

"I believe I will go too, squire, if you are not going to have too much of a load back," said Clark.

"You kin go as well as not, if you want to, but we'll all 'smell frost' before we git back home, you'd better believe!"

"I have my bear-skin robe to wrap up in, and your horses are fast travelers. I do not think that we will freeze in going fifteen miles."

"You must consider that we've got our road to break a good part of the way, my friend, and that makes the miles a heap longer."

Those persons who have never experienced a western winter can not realize how piercingly cold are the winds which sweep across the vast prairies with nothing to intercept them or break their force. A person dressed in ordinary winter clothing—overcoat and all— exposed upon the open country on a day when the mercury stands at fifteen or twenty degrees below zero, will feel very much as though he were clothed in garments of gauze. So our travelers incased themselves in their buffalo-robes and bear-skins, tied up their ears, gave a "last fond look" at the blazing fire and cheery room, and started.

All that day the kitchen was filled with the bustle of preparation, for, as Mrs. Hosmar said, the next was to be devoted to "moving," and no cooking could be done; and the one after was Christmas, and they were to have about twenty guests to dinner; so cake, and pies, and doughnuts, and trifles, and bread accumulated upon the shelves and tables—coffee was roasted, chickens and turkeys were dressed and hung up in the cellar, and every thing was done that could be done.

As evening drew near, there was much running to the windows and watching for the expected sleigh. Mrs. Boker prepared an extra nice supper, in honor of the expected daughter, and the boys kept piling wood upon the fire, until, in spite of winter weather, the whole house was filled with light and warmth.

But, alas, for waiting suppers! They are sure to spoil, and so did Mrs. Boker's. The short-cake got cold; the coffee boiled itself to death; the venison-steaks dried up, and refused to be juicy and tender any longer. Impatience was turned into anxiety; snow-drifts and "break-downs" became the topics of conversation, and inquiring eyes were constantly turned toward the staid old clock upon the mantle, which ticked away with perfect unconcern, seeming to be even more deliberate than usual, until finally it struck nine, just as a loud "hello!" at the door announced the tardy arrival.

Poke and Sam sprung out to take care of the horses, and in another moment, a dumpy figure, so bundled up that it seemed a marvel that it could fly around so, burst into the house, and fell upon Mrs. Boker, with many kisses and exclamations, and "Oh dear, how *good* it seems to come home!"

Then the squire, and Mr. Hosmar, and Mr. Clark came in, loaded down with bundles and "robes," and parcels of every size, all of which were dumped in a promiscuous pile in one corner, while the bearers gathered round the welcome fire to "thaw out." When the brisk little figure finally emerged from its manifold wrappings, it was introduced to Mrs. Hosmar and Annie, as "My daughter Mary," by the pleased mother.

"Fiddlesticks, wife! What's the use of introducin' these two girls to one another? Why, Annie has heard you talk about Molly till she knows her full history from the day she cut her first caper; and Molly has asked me more questions to-day than thar is in the catechism— how *tall* Annie was; if she was so *dreadful* han'som; if she was *engaged,* an' how many dresses—"

"Now, pa, you *know* that ain't so! Don't you b'lieve a word he says, Miss Hosmar. 'Twas him that done all the talking. He didn't give me a chance to ask many questions. If I was to tell all he said, ma'd be jealous right off."

"You Molly! You'd better not try to make difficulty between yer ma an' me 'fore you've been home half an hour!"

Mr. Hosmar, having by this time warmed up his benumbed hands, unbuttoned his overcoat, and drew from an inside pocket a letter which he handed to Annie.

"Oh, thank you! I was almost afraid there was none for me," and after a few pleasant words to Mary, she retired to her own little retreat to read her welcome "news from a far country." Annie's face grew thoughtful and troubled as she read, and she murmured to herself as she slowly folded the closely written sheet. "Yes, I did wrong; he may not have realized how far he has carried his habit of interference and surveillance. I suppose his pet scheme occupied his mind so wholly that he could not bear to see a chance of its miscarrying. He may not have meant to be unkind; still, how *could* I endure it? But I will write to him. *Mamma* loved him, and trusted him, implicitly," and as she again unfolds the sheet to reperuse the letter, we will glance over the pages and see what her friend Susie Malor says:

DEAR ANNIE—I have only heard from you twice since you went away, but as you say that it is fifteen miles to the nearest post-office, I suppose I ought not to complain. And now, dear Annie, I must proceed at once to the subject nearest my heart. You know of old, that I am exceedingly frank and plain-spoken, and it is because I do really love you that I take the liberty of giving advice.

Well, then, I think that you ought to write to Mr. Norris, and let him know where you are, and with whom; he seems quite broken down and unhappy. There are persons who seem inclined to make a great mystery of your sudden disappearance from among us, and, according to Mrs. Plyne, he is much annoyed and mortified by being asked questions concerning you, which of course he is unable to answer. I had a long and pitiful recital of his troubles from Mrs. P. a few days ago; but what has most excited my sympathy for him is the careworn and anxious expression that has settled upon his countenance. I know that you had cause to feel aggrieved and indignant, but I really wish that you had taken some other way of escaping from the unpleasantness of your position.

Mr. Norris is too dignified to question me very closely, but Mrs. Plyne asked me "point-blank" if I knew who it was that you went with. I told her, with as innocent an air as possible, that "a colored man came for you in a carriage, and that he seemed to be one with whom you were well acquainted." I haven't the least talent for prevarication, and I think that I was strongly suspected of "squibing," and nothing would give me greater pleasure than to see you safely at home again, etc., etc., etc.

Early in the forenoon of the day following, the squire's famous oxen were hitched to the great sled, and "gee-hawed" around to the door, and the work of loading on the goods to be moved was begun; and before night came, the Hosmars were comfortably settled in their new home. Poor, tired, meek Mrs. Hosmar, although generally prone to look upon the dark side of things, could but give a sigh of content and satisfaction, when, every thing in its place, she looked around and realized that 'twas all their own—they were once more at *home!*

Mr. Hosmar and the boys gathered around the blazing fire in the kitchen, while Mrs. Hosmar cleared away the supper dishes.

"I tell you what 'tis, Rachel. This is better than living in somebody else's house, isn't it?"

"Why, yes; a body feels so much more independent. The squire and his wife was both as kind and as clever as folks *could* be, but I allers felt as if we was a-puttin' 'em out too much, bein' as we was strangers to 'em—no kin or any thing!"

"Wal, yes; but that wasn't what I meant exactly. Me an' the boys kin do many a good turn fur Squire Boker in the course of the year, an' I intend to pay off fur all he's done fur us; but you know before we came West we always lived on somebody else's land and farmed it on the sheers, or paid rent fur it, an' now we're in a house of our own, and hev got land of our own, and land that's worth plowin', too. I tell you it makes a man feel as if he was somebody!"

Mrs. Boker, Mary and Annie—who had remained as visitor for a day or two—also had a busy day putting things "to rights," and restoring the house to its usual order, after the departure of the other family; but by sunset every thing was arranged in its accustomed place; a bright fire flamed upon the neatly-swept hearth, the supper-table, with its snow-white cloth, stood ready to receive the smoking and substantial meal which was to atone for the cold "lunch" which had, that day, take the place of the usual dinner. Mrs. Boker was resting her weary self in the arm-chair, while Mary was making the final preparations for supper.

"Now, ma, supper's ready, and here comes pa and Mr. Clark. I'll light a candle, and then we'll set down."

"I reckon I'd better not tell 'em the news till after supper; it might spile their appetites," remarked the squire, glancing around at Mr. Clark, as though seeking his advice on the subject.

"I am sorry you have mentioned it, squire; I don't like to think about it myself, though I am not quite vain enough to suppose it likely to injure any one's appetite but my own."

"If it is very affecting news, pa, you'd better keep it a spell, for I can't afford to lose my dinner and supper both!" spoke up Mary, gayly.

Annie looked toward Mr. Clark with an almost unconsciously inquiring gaze, and found him regarding her with a wistful expression in his dark-blue eyes, which sent a faint tinge of color to her brow, and caused her hand to tremble slightly as she received her cup of coffee from Mrs. Boker, who, glancing first at her husband, and then at Mr. Clark, exclaimed:

"You might as well tell us now. I kin guess what it is, though. Mr. Clark is a-goin' away—ain't that it?"

"You're right, wife, an' if Molly here hadn't a-come home jest as she did, we'd a-been left as forlorn as an orphanless widder."

"How did you come to take sech a sudden notion, Mr. Clark? I thought you was a-goin' to stay here with us till spring!" asked Mrs. Boker.

"Well, indeed, Mrs. Boker, I *should* have gone on in the fall, as soon as I was well enough to do so; now my business partner writes that I *must* come. I received letters yesterday that accuse me of gross neglect of duty in wasting so much time; and, as my conscience does not plead 'not guilty,' I suppose I must obey the summons at once."

"Wal, we'll all be sorry to hev you leave us, but if you must, why you must, I reckon!" said Mrs. Boker, with a sigh.

"Oh, you needn't feel so bad, wife; he's a-comin' back ag'in."

"Is that so?" exclaimed Mrs. Boker, with an involuntary glance at Annie.

Mr. Clark observed the look, and understood it. So did the squire, who remarked, in a dry sort of way:

"You know he's been lookin' round the country considerable sence he's been here, and he's bought up right smart of land—of course he'll hev to come out an' look after it."

"And perhaps bring out a colony of New Englanders to settle on it," added Clark, quietly. "There is a beautiful site for a town near the creek, with water enough for a mill or two, and timber sufficient to build the houses, and a soil richer than any of them ever dreamed of."

"Be sure and heve a smart lot of young men amongst them, then. Beaux are dreadful scarce out here," added Mary, with a little laugh.

"Oh yes! I'd be willin' to testify that the first spruce Yankee that might come along with a one-horse wagon full of wooden nutmegs to peddle round 'mongst us, would be the very feller *you'd* fall in love with, Miss Molly. Now, I hate them slick Yankees—"

"Why, pa, you forgit that Mr. Clark is a Yankee, don't you?" said Mary, roguishly.

"Wal, he don't b'long to the breed I'm talkin' about; an' besides that, he's been 'round the world a heap, an' is considerable ahead of any other Yankee ever I heerd of."

"You will change your mind about the New Englanders if some of them should chance to find their way into this neighborhood. In a few years you would see yourself surrounded by a thriving, enterprising community—here a school-house, there a church, your prairie dotted with beautiful groves and thrifty orchards. I acknowledge that the unmitigated Yankee has some very small-sized ideas; but take an eastern man, and westernize him, and you have one of the very best specimens of an American man," said Clark.

"I reckon you don't intend to start fur a few days yit, do you?" inquired Mrs. Boker.

"I must help you celebrate Christmas, and then, if the weather will permit traveling, I must go."

"Yes, Jane, I've promised to start with him day-after-to-morrow,

and take him as fur as Council Bluffs. There he kin take the stage for
St. Louis. It'll take me two days to git to the Bluffs, an' two to come
back. So you see you are going to lose us both at once!"

"We'll be dretful lonesome, that's certain, havin' so many leave us
all at one time. But how do you calculate to go?"

"Clark an' me has been overhaulin' the old one-horse sleigh, an'
tinkerin' it up a little, so't I reckon it'll hold together. Clark, you'd
better drive over to Hosmar's in it to-morrow an' git Poke to put in a
brace or two; he kin do more towards fixin' it up in ten minutes than
we could by fussin' over it all day."

"That is a good idea, squire; I would really like to drive Gentle-
Mike once more; and if I never return to the West, I give him to you;
but take good care of him, for he and I are good friends."

"Wal, drive him to-morrow. You kin take Annie over; she'd
ruther hev a *sleigh*-ride than a *sled*-ride, I know."

Christmas morning came with the promise of a pleasant day, and
long before sunrise, the family at the new house was all up and astir.
Jim and Johnny were the first out of bed. No considerations of
comfort or propriety could restrain their impatience to learn what was
in store for them in the way of Christmas gifts; so without waiting to
put on their clothes, but with their garments in their hands, they
tumbled down the stairs, and rushed through the cold and dark into
the kitchen. After a hasty fumble, and the discovery that there really *was*
something for them, they concluded to have a light before making any
further investigations; so the ashes were quickly raked off the bed of
fiery coals upon the hearth; the dry kindlings, close at hand, were
thrown on, and soon a bright and cheerful blaze revealed to the
delighted eyes of the eager boys, the treasures of Christmas-morn.
There were candy and nuts, and little fanciful cakes in every
conceivable shape; there was in each hat a pair of knit mittens in red
and blue and white diamonds, and—better than all—just under each
pair, lay a good, serviceable pocket-knife—"the *very thing* I wanted!"
cried each one exultingly—and then there was a hasty putting on of

trowsers, the first need of them experienced, being, a pocket to put the knife in.

"Poke thinks that nobody didn't get any thing but him, I reckon!" said Jake, glancing significantly at Poke's feet, which were thrust rather conspicuously forward into the light of the fire.

"De fac' is," said Poke, complacently, "dese boots *do* suit me mos' awful well. Massa Clark's a mighty nice man; heap of gentleman 'bout *him*. Didn't use to like him so *berry* much, but, we's all reliable to be mistaken on firs' acquaintance."

"Oh, he's bully, I tell *you!*" responded Jake. "He told me yesterday, 'fore we come over here, how to manage it—to take yer old boots away after you was asleep, an' set *them* in their place, so't when you got up in the mornin' you'd put 'em on 'fore you knowed it—an' 'twas me that got yer measure fur him 'fore he went to town, so that they'd be sure an' fit—an' he give *me* a silver dollar to spend fur jest whatever I've a mind to!"

"Wal, dese is a fit, sure enough!" replied Poke, eying his monstrous feet with evident delight.

"Wal, now, come to yer breakfasts, all of ye—I'm in a dretful hurry, fur it's time them turkeys was a parboilin', an' the mornin' is slippin' away powerful fast."

About ten o'clock, Gentle-Mike was hitched to the sleigh in which Annie was to be taken over to her new home. He was a beautiful animal, perfectly gentle and well-trained. His glossy brown coat was like satin; his delicate and pointed ears seemed quivering with animation; his large bright eyes were expressive of spirit and intelligence; his nostrils were thin and glowing; no wonder that his master loved him, nor that he stopped to give him an affectionate caress, as he enjoined him to stand very quiet until all were ready to go. The bear-skin robe was brought out and placed in the sleigh; then a bundle was stowed carefully away under the seat; and finally Mr. Clark and Annie came out, followed to the door by Mrs. Boker and Mary.

"This is a splendid morning for a sleigh-ride!" called out Mary, as Mr. Clark seated himself in the sleigh, and began to tuck the furs around Annie. "If I was in your place I'd go on down the creek an' meet the folks that's comin' up to Hosmar's."

"It *is* a pleasant morning, and if Miss Annie does not object we *will* drive on a few miles; the sleighing is prime!" said Mr. Clark, glancing at Annie inquiringly.

"Gentle-Mike looks as though *he* would like it!" said Annie

"But would *you*—*that* is the question," said Clark in a low voice.

"Oh, yes indeed! I love a good sleigh-ride when it is not too cold—especially with such a horse as this!" was the gay reply.

"Well, then, Mrs. Boker," said Mr. Clark, "if we are not at Mr. Hosmar's when you arrive there, don't think that I have run away with the sleigh, nor that we are lost in the snow. We will be sure to be there before dinner."

"Better take another shawl to wrap up in if you're a-goin' to ride fur, hadn't you Annie?" said Mrs. Boker

"Oh no! It is not very cold to-day, and Mr. Clark will not drive far I suppose; we shall be at auntie's almost as soon as you."

"Well then, Mike, you may go!" said the driver, and in a moment they were gliding rapidly away over the snow-covered prairie.

"How bright and cheerful the world looks this morning," said Annie, as they turned toward the creek. "Christmas is the holiday of holidays to me, and I do love to see the sun shine on it!"

" 'Tis the flavor of our childhood's beliefs and enjoyments of it, still clinging around it, which constitutes the charm, I suppose," said Mr. Clark.

"Partly so. Santa Claus is a 'bona fide' personage in *my* eyes yet; I can't bear to give him up! I could not help thinking, as we sat around the fire last evening, what a good wide chimney there was for the old fellow to come down without the least danger of a tight squeeze to his pack, and I was nearly tempted to hang my stockings in the corner!" said Annie, with a gay laugh.

"If I had but known it, *I* might have acted the part of the good saint. I had a package of bon-bons in store for the boys."

"They have cause to rejoice, then, that their privileges have not been usurped! But there comes a sled-load of the down-the-creek guests, I believe!"

"Why yes! That is Mr. Wilson and his family; but we will take our drive still, unless you wish to return at once. It is not yet eleven o'clock, and we have an abundance of time."

"I am enjoying the ride and do not object in the least to another mile or so!" replied Annie, frankly, and then, seeing Mr. Clark's face light up with a pleased smile, she blushed, and began to feel indignant.

"The conceited fellow," she thought. "I'll warrant he thinks it's himself that I am pleased with instead of the ride!" and for a time her gayety was lost, and she scarcely responded a word to the remarks made by her escort.

At length the silence became mutual. Mr. Clark could not understand the sudden change in his companion's manner; he felt troubled and embarrassed, but resolved to "say his say." The time was short—the opportunity, perhaps, his last—and he began:

"Miss Annie, whither have your spirits flown? A few moments ago you were as blithe as a bird; now you seem sunk in despondency or displeasure. I am at a loss to know which."

"Neither, Mr. Clark. I was but reflecting upon the vanity of mankind."

"I am doubtless dull of comprehension, for I really do not understand the matter at all; but I have something to say to you which I fear may not be very pleasant for you to hear, but I *must* say it while I have an opportunity.

"You know that I expect to leave this place to-morrow, to return to the East, and I wish to say to you before I go, that—that I *love* you—that the dearest desire of my heart is to win you for my wife. I have never presumed to think that you cared for *me,* and if I had not been going away, I should not yet have spoken."

"Mr. Clark," began Annie, but he immediately interrupted her:

"Do not say any thing now. I can not bear to hear you declare that you care nothing for me, although I fear that you do not; but, will you allow me to write to you? Will not you answer my letters?"

There was no reply, and Mr. Clark resumed:

"I shall come back here next summer, and if, as I hope, you will permit me to write to you during my absence, our acquaintance will grow—perhaps you will *learn* to love me."

There was such a pleading earnestness in the speaker's voice, that Annie's indignation subsided into some kinder feeling, and she answered, gently:

"I can not make any promises, Mr. Clark. I do *not* love you; we are but little more than strangers to each other. How have I led you to think—"

"You never have; I did not presume to imagine that you loved me: I only ask to be remembered. I will come again; the future is always full of hope and promise; perhaps it holds the blessing of your love for me."

"I think we have gone as far as we ought, Mr. Clark; please turn Mike's head toward home."

"In another moment I will; but first say if I may not write to you—if you will not wear this ring? *Not* as a symbol or a pledge, but merely as a remembrancer of me."

"I can not wear the ring. I do not wish you to think that I shall *ever* love you; but, if you wish to write to me, I will read and answer your letters with pleasure, provided they are not 'love-letters,'" she added, trying to regain the former gayety of her tones.

Gentle-Mike was now turned homeward, and he was rapidly nearing Mr. Hosmar's, before either one spoke again, and then Mr. Clark said:

"We are *friends* at least, and I must be content to *wait;* but I have faith and hope to fortify me against despair, or even despondency."

As they drove up to the door, Poke came out to take charge of

Gentle-Mike, and his broad smile and zealous attentions to both horse and master were a cause of wonder to Annie, who had not yet heard the story of the boots.

The "house-warming" went off with entire success. The guests were all in a good humor, and seemed bent upon enjoying themselves; the dinner was bountiful and worthy of the occasion; the youngsters were abundantly supplied with candies, nuts, and various sorts of confectionery, Mr. Clark and Annie having, each of them, made special provision for that part of the entertainment; and Squire Boker seemed over-flowing with jokes and jollity.

Mr. Clark sung several popular songs in his very best style, and was applauded and admired to such a degree, that in sheer self-defense he was obliged to suggest Poke and his banjo, as a substitute for himself, in the way of musical entertainment. The squire "seconded this motion" with great promptness and energy, but Poke retained his seat by the kitchen-fire, and was not to be persuaded to show off his accomplishments "before folks." In vain Mary teased and her father exhorted; in vain the company declared that they had never seen or heard a banjo, and were "most uncommon" anxious to do so; in vain the boys brought forth the instrument and endeavored to put it in his hands: he remained as stolid and immovable as a lay figure, and was, to all intents and purposes, deaf, dumb, and blind.

Finally the squire turned away with an expression of unmitigated disgust upon his countenance, and returned to the sitting-room, where he sought out Annie.

"See here, Miss Annie," he began, "we want you to come out into the kitchen, an' see what *you* kin do with that obstinate darky. We've been a-tryin' to coax him to give us a little tune or two, but thar he sets an' won't even wink! I'm willin' to swear that he comes the neardest to bein' a mule of any human I ever happened to come acrost yit! But ef *anybody* kin git him to do it, it's you; he generally knocks under when *you* take him in hand, though he's a *leetle* inclined to *go slow*, you know. But, try him, fur pity's sake. The very idea of the music that's a-stickin' in that old banjo, an' nothin' but a little thumpin' wantin' to bring it out, is enough to make a fellow obstreperous!"

"I feel really sorry for you, squire," replied Annie, laughingly, "and will see what can be done, but the company must congregate in this room. He will remain as immovable as a stone as long as all those strangers are around him."

"Wal, then I'll hev 'em out of thar in less than no time. I'll git Clark to sing the 'Californy Diggers,' *that'll* bring 'em in here like a swarm of bees round a posy-bed when the jew is on."

So saying, the squire walked off to secure Mr. Clark's cooperation, and soon, as was expected, the kitchen was deserted by every one but Poke, who retained his rigidity until Annie came out and closed the door between the two rooms. She carried a parcel in her hands, and advancing toward the fire, said, pleasantly:

"Aunt Rachel tells me that you had a Christmas present this morning, Poke."

" 'Deed I did, Miss Annie! Dese yer boots was a-standin' in de place of de ole ones when I got up dis mornin'. I 'spects Massa Clark's a mighty nice man. Berry sorry I ebber had sich a prejudice ag'in' him. I use' to t'ink he wasn't nobody of any 'count, but de squire says he made a heap of money w'ile he was in Californy, 'sides bein' a lawyer, an' b'longin' to one of de fuss fam'lies up north."

"Well, Poke, I have something for you, too. I've been waiting for an opportunity to give it to you; here it is," and she handed him the package which she had been holding. Poke took it with a delighted grin, and turned it over two or three times without attempting to undo it, until Annie exclaimed:

"Why don't you look to see what it is? I don't believe you care about *my* present."

"Now, Miss Annie, you know dat ain't so!" expostulated Poke, unwrapping the paper. "I's *berry* much obliged to ye. Why, Miss Annie, ef here ain't two shirts! Linen bosoms all plaited as fine as—an' a west! Why, Miss Annie, but dis is a mos' *splendid* west—*welwet,* ain't it, now?"

and Poke held aloft the gorgeous red-and-yellow-flowered garment in an ecstasy of admiration.

"I want you to put it on, so that I can see how you look in it—now, while the door is closed, and the company is in the other room."

Poke hurriedly arrayed himself in the new vest, and then strutted across the room to the little square looking-glass which hung against the wall, and surveyed himself with undisguised admiration.

"Now," said Annie, "feel in the watch-pocket; you will find something in it."

Poke thrust his fingers into the pocket and drew forth a bright, new five-dollar gold-piece, lightly wrapped in a piece of tissue-paper.

" 'Deed, Miss Annie, you is *too* good. I's afeered I can't nebber pay up fur all dese—"

"The money is to put with your savings, Poke, not to spend; and I owed you something for fixing up my room so nicely. Now, put on your coat and take your banjo; I'm going to sing a song or two to gratify these people, and I want you to help me."

A dubious and perplexed expression flitted across the dusky countenance, and mingled with the broad smile which still lingered there, but a glance at the resplendent vest and the glittering coin in his fingers, banished all but the smile, and he replaced his coat with alacrity, took up his banjo, and said:

"What is you a-goin' to sing, missus?"

"You taught me half a dozen songs when I was a child. We used to sing them together under the great apple-tree which shaded the kitchen-door. We have not sung them together for years, but I remember them perfectly, and I know that you do, for I heard you humming my old favorite, 'Before the Cabin Door,' only a few days ago. We will try that first. I will open the door, and when they hear the banjo I presume they will all come out here, but you need not look at them or think of them at all: we will sing just as we used to do under the old apple-tree."

Annie then opened the door between the two rooms, and Poke

struck a few notes of a prelude, which proved a signal for a rush to the scene of action, and in a moment the whole party was gathered in the ample kitchen. Poke had a peculiarly rich, mellow voice, exactly suited to the simple melodies of his race, and Annie's clear, alto tones were sweet and well trained, and the little audience of uncritical pioneers were fairly enchanted, and thought that they had never heard *real music* before.

Squire Boker was passionately fond of music; it seemed to stir up all the tender emotions of his soul, and he listened to the singers with a delight that seemed almost childish; and when they sung a little song for their last, which had just a "touch" of the pathetic in it, he was obliged to resort to the time-honored custom of blowing the nose in the most vigorous and stentorian manner, in order to conceal his emotion. In fact, Mary openly declared, as soon as the song was finished, that "Pa was a-crying."

"*Crying,* indeed!" said her father. "Jest as if a fellow couldn't blow his nose on Christmas without being accused of boo-hoo-in'. Now, if *you* could sing like *that,* Miss Molly, you'd be good for something!"

"Wal, husband," said Mrs. Boker, "it's purty near four o'clock, an' I reckon we'd better be a-fixin' to start home."

"We must go, too," remarked Mr. Wilson. "It'll be dark, now, afore we kin git home. Git yer duds on, wife. I'll be round to the door with the sled in less'n ten minutes."

And so the new house of the prairie-settler was "warmed," and so seemed to be too some of the hearts which gathered in it, for, as the guests departed, there was much shaking of hands and many injunctions to "be neighborly," and "sociable," and "not to stand on ceremony, but come jest whenever you kin," so that the Hosmars began to feel as though they had gained both friends and home.

Mr. Clark did not seek to say a special "good-by" to Annie. He spoke cheerfully of "hoping to see them all again before another Christmas should come round," and then, with a final "good-by, all!" sprung into his sleigh, took possession of the lines, spoke a word or two of Mike, and glided swiftly away.

CHAPTER SEVEN

THE STORM-VICTIM

Squire Boker's family were "up and doing," long before daylight upon the morning after Christmas, and the substantial and smoking-hot breakfast was partaken of by candle-light that the final preparations for the journey to Council Bluffs might be completed in good season for the travelers to have the advantage of an "early start."

But the aspect of matters out of doors seemed decidedly unpropitious; the air was damp, and a chilling wind blew strongly from the south-west; not a speck of blue sky was to be seen; all was dull, gray, and lowering. So the breakfast was lingered over, and the weather discussed until the tardy morning had advanced to sunrise.

"I tell you what 'tis, Clark," said the squire, glancing out of the window. "I don't b'lieve thar's any use in our thinkin' about startin' out to-day; it's my opinion that it'll either rain or snow, before two hours, an' to start across the prairie on sich a trip in oncertain weather, would be most uncommon foolish. I reckon you'll hev to hold on a while till this spell of weather fizzles out!"

"As I am anxious to be on my way as soon as possible, I think I will venture to go as far as Blufftown this afternoon, if it does not rain so as to melt all the snow off the ground. If you are willing to part with your sleigh, squire, I will take Gentle-Mike and go to Council Bluffs alone. I can leave the horse with some one there until an opportunity occurs to have him sent back to you."

After some further discussion, the plan was finally agreed upon. As the day advanced, it appeared to grow rather colder, and instead of rain came little blustering snow-squalls; but about noon the clouds grew thinner and higher, and the wind almost ceased to blow. Mr. Clark thought that he would gain nothing by waiting, and so, immediately after dinner, Gentle-Mike was harnessed and driven around to the door; the bear-skin robe, and kind Mrs. Boker's inevitable hot stone, were placed in the sleigh, and, after a lingering hand-shaking and reiterated good-byes, the young man departed.

For an hour or two after noon, the sun seemed to be making an effort to dispel the clouds and cheer the world below; but then the clouds grew denser, the wind rose, the snow began to whirl through the air with a violence peculiar to western snow-storms, and the temperature grew rapidly lower, until it seemed a wonder that it *could* snow.

In the course of half-an-hour from the time the storm began it would have been unsafe to venture out of doors; the air was literally full of snow—fine, icy, whirling, penetrating snow. The wind kept that which was falling—or trying to fall—in the air, and also took that which had once been on the ground, and kept it in circulation, likewise. A person exposed to such a storm, would be liable to become utterly confused and lost, and perhaps perish, when not a rod from shelter and safety.

Mr. and Mrs. Boker grew seriously alarmed for Mr. Clark's welfare.

"I'd give my best yoke of oxen ef he hadn't a-started," exclaimed the squire at last, walking to the window and gazing at the tempest without.

"I do wish we'd a-persuaded him to a-waited," replied his wife. "He'll be most certain to perish unless he reached a stoppin' place afore this storm broke loose!"

The afternoon wore away, night fell, and still the tempest raged.

Windows and doors shivered and rattled; the roof creaked, the fine snow sifted in at unseen crevices, and the wind seemed to penetrate the very walls.

Father, mother, and daughter were seated closely around the blazing fire. The two women were knitting silently, and the squire, with his boots off, was toasting his feet upon the hearth, and indulging in a doze. The old clock upon the mantle struck seven, when a heavy thump against the side of the house caused Mary and her mother to spring to their feet.

"What was it, ma?" exclaimed Mary.

"The dear only knows. Wake yer pa."

The squire came out of his doze with an effort and, in a bewildered sort of way, inquired dreamily:

"Has Clark come?"

Just then the sharp whinny of a horse was heard at the door, and the squire, fairly aroused, hastily pulled on his boots and without stopping to put on his hat, hurried out, followed to the door by Mary, who peered out into the storm, anxious to know what was the matter; but the snow whirled into her face, preventing her from making any discoveries, until her father's voice was heard exclaiming:

"I vow! If this ain't Mike an' the sleigh!"

Mrs. Boker and Mary both came out upon the steps.

"Molly, you go in and hold a light to the window. I don't b'lieve the sleigh's empty after all."

Mary ran in, and held the candle up to the window near which the sleigh stood; for Mike had swung the vehicle against the house when he stopped.

"Jane, Molly—*he's here!* Froze dead, I'm afraid! In God's name, help! Help!"

By the united efforts of the three, the miserable man was carried into the house and laid upon the bed.

"Whisky in the closet, Mary; bring it, and that bundle of old flannel on the shelf!"

These orders were issued while the cramped and stiffened limbs were being straightened, and their covering removed. Then blankets were brought, and a course of rubbing with flannel cloths wet in whisky begun, and kept up, until signs of returning consciousness appeared.

"Now a little whisky in his mouth!"

This was done, and repeated every few moments, and the friction kept up, till great drops of sweat rolled down the anxious faces of the two earnest workers.

"Pa, poor Mike is a-whinnyin' at the door; he oughtn't to stand there in the cold after such a run," said Mary.

"That's so, Molly, but I can't 'tend to him *now.*"

"I'll take a buffalo-robe out, an' put over him."

"A good notion, Molly. He's a human beast."

Finally the life which had been almost chilled out returned; but days of suffering, languor, and prostration followed.

The storm lasted all that night, and until near noon the next day; then the wind lulled, and the sun shone forth in unobscured glory. Clark lay in a sort of stupor, only occasionally seeming fully conscious, and speaking a few feeble words. The squire hovered around the bed, like a mother over the cradle of a sick child.

About the middle of the afternoon the sufferer awoke from a lethargic sleep, and as soon as his wakefulness was observed, the squire went to his bedside.

"Any thing I kin do fur ye, Clark?"

The young man looked at the kind face bent over him, for a moment, in silence, and with eyes of glittering brightness, then asked:

"Has Annie come yet?"

"Why no; I didn't know you wanted her sent fur."

"Then she has perished—perished!"

"She's safe at home, friend; what do ye mean? Jane, come here; I b'lieve Clark's out of his head!"

"Mike was dragging her through the snow—and it was so

cold—so cold! He wouldn't stop—I tried to follow—but the drifts were so deep."

"Mike's in the stable, an' Annie is snug an' warm at home. You mustn't git sich crooked notions in yer head, man," said the squire, soothingly, but the expression of the glassy eyes did not change, and Mrs. Boker remarked:

"He's feverish; he'll be apt to be flighty fur a spell. I wish, though, she wus here; it might keep him from worryin' if he wus to see her 'round."

"I'll take the sleigh and go after her ef you think so."

"I'm afeerd she wouldn't come; some girls is so curious."

"*She* ain't, though. She's got more sense, an' independence enough to make a Fourth-o'-July celebration of! I'll go right off. The snow is drifted with young mountains, but I reckon I kin git through it, or around it."

Annie came; and good Mrs. Boker met her upon the steps, to give a few words of explanation.

"He's a leetle flight by spells—seems to think you're in danger or distress somewhere; so we thought if you wus to come over where he could see you fur himself, mebbe 'twould quiet him off, or save him from frettin' himself into a fever."

"Well, here I am, and willing to do all the good I can. Is he awake?"

"I b'lieve he is. Now you jist go in, an' walk right up an' speak to him. Mary waits on him as if he wus her brother!"

Annie understood the kindly consideration which prompted the last clause, and could not refrain from a smile. Prudery was no part of her composition.

Mr. Clark appeared to sleep, and Annie sat down by the fire. Mary came quietly, and relieved her of her wrappings with only a whispered greeting. But when the squire returned from the stable, with his louder step and more noisy movements, the sleeper aroused, and asked the same question as before:

"Has Annie come?"

Annie immediately went to the bedside, and leaning toward him, said, gently:

"Here I am. What shall I do for you?"

He looked at her with an inquiring and perplexed gaze for a moment; then the expression of doubt and uncertainty changed to one of rapture and delight. He reached forth both his hands, took one of hers and pressed it to his lips, and murmured, "She is safe—safe!" Then, with a sigh of perfect content, he sunk into sleep again.

Annie softly drew her hand away and stole back to the fire. Her eyes were full of tears, and her heart beat so rapidly that, for a few moments, she could scarcely breathe; and with an open book to screen her face from the fire, and from observation, she sat and pondered.

"Am I really so much to this man? If he loves me, he loves me for myself alone. I am not Annie Howard the heiress, to *him*. Perhaps—" But what else she thought must be left to conjecture.

About two weeks after the catastrophe of the snow-storm, Mr. Hosmar proposed to his wife and Annie to spend the evening at the Bokers'.

"The squire says Clark ain't well enough to venture out yit, an' is dreatful lonesome an' oneasy like; he thinks a little company would cheer him up; so ef thar's nothing in the way, we'll go over after supper."

"Nothing that I know of. I shall be glad of the chance fur my part. What do *you* say, Annie?"

"I will go, of course, auntie. It won't do to refuse invitations when they are so 'few and far between,'" was the laughing reply.

So, by "early candlelight," the neighbors were chatting together around a cheerful fire at the squire's. Mr. Clark was seated in the "old arm-chair," looking as pale and "interesting" as any hero could desire. Annie was patiently initiating Mary into the mysteries of some new "stitch" in fancy knitting, while the two elder ladies were engaged in discussing the merits and demerits of "cross-band" and "double–an'–twisted."

"I don't b'lieve I ever heerd you tell how you happened to git back here that night, Clark," said Mr. Hosmar.

" 'Twas Mike's sagacity that brought me here," replied the young man. "In less than an hour after I started away it began to storm. I thought at first 'twas but a squall, and would soon be over; then, as the snow came faster and faster, and the wind grew colder and colder, I began to realize that my situation was becoming perilous. I urged Mike on, thinking that I might soon find shelter, but the wind was in my face; the air was thick with snow, and I soon became perfectly bewildered, and uncertain whither I was going. But we went on, and on, until I knew that we had had more than time to reach Bluffton. I saw, too, that the short winter afternoon was drawing to a close, and felt that I was approaching a critical point. I slapped my hands together and stamped my feet, as long as I had power to move them; then a drowsy indifference to consequences took possession of me, and I got down into the body of the sleigh, as well as I could; pulled the bear-skin over me, and left Mike to take his own course. The faithful creature brought me here, and I am again indebted to these good friends of mine for the best of nursing and the kindest care."

"Oh yes! But then a certain young lady had to be sent for before you'd b'lieve 'twasn't *her* that needed takin' care of, instid of yerself; or, did you jest purtend that, so't I'd go an' bring her over for you to look at?" said the squire, jocosely.

"I remember a sort of horrid nightmare, in which I seemed to see Miss Annie struggling through mountain-like snow-drifts, while I was unable to advance a step to her assistance; but I was not aware, until now, that I made my feverish fancies known."

CHAPTER EIGHT

WON

Several weeks of convalescence followed Mr. Clark's unfortunate ride. A mild and almost spring-like February succeeded the cold and stormy month of January, and there seemed no longer any impediment in the way of the long-declared return to the East; but some charm seemed to hold the young man back, and 'twas not until the middle of the month that he again made preparations for the journey.

Upon the afternoon previous to his intended departure, he walked over to the "new house" to bid good-by to his friends there. A soft and delicate green was already beginning to appear upon the prairie. The sky was blue and cloudless, the sun shone cheerily, and the out-of-door air was so pleasant, that, after a few moments' conversation with Mr. and Mrs. Hosmar, and a short frolic with the youngsters, he proposed to Annie that they should go out for a walk; and the two were soon strolling along toward the bluffs which rose about half-a-mile beyond the house.

"And you are really going, to-morrow?" asked Annie.

"Yes, I am *really* going in the morning, unless something altogether unforeseen occurs to prevent; and I must tell you now, before I forget it, that Mrs. Boker sent an urgent request by me that you would spend the time of the squire's absence with her. She says that you are 'sech good company.'"

"Quite a compliment. But, seriously, good, kind Mrs. Boker is one of my best friends, and I love her dearly!"

"*Love her,* Annie! Oh, what would I not give to hear you say that of *me!*"

Annie blushed, smiled, and began: "Well then—" but her voice faltered and failed, and she never completed the sentence; but her companion seemed to be very much delighted with the two little words she *did* speak, or something connected with them, and when, an hour or two afterward, they turned their steps homeward, a little ring sparkled upon one of Annie's fingers, which had never been there before.

"And now I must tell you, dear Annie, what you ought to have known before—that the name which will be yours by-and-by, is not *Clark*, but *Norris*. I—"

The look of surprise, consternation, and bewilderment which flitted across the countenance he was regarding so tenderly and proudly, caused the speaker to pause abruptly.

"Why, Annie, dear Annie! How pale you are! I had no idea you could be so shocked. Let me hasten to explain. 'Twas only my carelessness which caused me to allow such a misunderstanding to continue. Squire Boker has known from our first acquaintance, that 'Clark' was but one of my 'given' names; Charles Clark Norris is the whole name. Indeed, Annie, you look so strangely that I feel as though I had been guilty of a serious offense—a grave misdemeanor—an unpardonable deception!"

"I am surprised, of course," said Annie, and her face was now aglow with color, while an expression of half-comical distress settled upon it for a few moments; then a ringing laugh burst forth, and she exclaimed—"'What's in a name!' Go on, Mr. Charles Clark Norris, with your confession!" and another merry laugh followed.

"I am not *confessing;* only 'stating the case'; and your mirthful tones reassure me wonderfully! Well, then, there were three young men of us went from Thurston together. We were intimate friends, and all 'Charlies.' I was the only one of the trio who rejoiced in two appellations besides our surnames. We were Charlie Souther, Charlie Upton and Charlie Clark Norris. After spending a year and a half in California, we, with ten others whose acquaintance we had formed, concluded, for the sake of adventure, to come home across the plains. Singularly enough there were two more Charlies in the band, and, as we were all upon familiar terms, there soon grew to be a perfect medley of Charlies; so we three finally agreed upon a plan to distinguish ourselves from the others. The first was to respond only when spoken to as 'Souther;' the second declared he would be nothing else but 'Peter,' and so we continued to call him during the remainder of the journey. Fortunately, I had something to fall back upon, and suggested 'Clark'—'Norris' not being eligible as there were two brothers in the company named Norse, and the two names were pronounced so nearly alike, that it would have been but little more distinctive than the first.

"The journey across the plains was harder work than we expected to find it; we met with privations and toils that were not down in our programme. We also had two or three skirmishes with the Indians, and by the time we reached this place, the surplus energy with which we started out was quite exhausted. We made our camp and were determined to rest and recruit our strength, and, as our captain said, 'slick up a little.' By the time the rest of the company were ready to go on I was attacked by a fever, and was obliged to accept Squire Boker's kind proposal that I should remain with him until I recovered my health. He, hearing all of my companions address me as 'Clark,' supposed of course that it was my family-name, and although I undeceived him after going into his house, he never seemed to remember, and I have been 'Mr.' Clark ever since a kind fate left me here to find *you!*"

"Clark" at last was really gone and had been heard from as having safely arrived at his destination in the East. A letter to "Miss Annie Hosmar" duly announced that fact.

The winter sped rapidly, and Poke, who had learned the way to Blufftown, was the bearer of numerous missives. Those which went eastward always were signed simply "Annie."

One day in the latter part of March, a letter came from Mrs. Plyne—for Annie had written her soon after Christmas—which urged her immediate return home if the weather was such as would permit of comfortable traveling. "Father and I will meet you at St. Louis; the spring is unusually early, and the boats are already running. We are at a loss to know how you will get so far as that alone, but hope you will be able to find a protector. Father would take the whole journey in order to accompany you home, but his health is very feeble, and he is altogether unable to endure so much fatigue. I am in hopes that the trip to St. Louis, and seeing you safely at home again, may revive his spirits and help to restore his health." Such was the tenor of Mrs. Plyne's letter. Annie felt grieved and remorseful as she thought of her stepfather's declining health.

"I will write to them at once, and tell them that I will begin my journey homeward as soon as I think they have had time to receive my letter. They can then be in St. Louis in advance of my arrival there. Poke seems homesick, and no doubt will be glad to return to Kentucky. He will be all the 'protector' I shall need."

Thus mused Annie, as she sat at her south window, with the recently-perused letter in her hand. Then her thoughts wandered to another subject. She held up her little hand to gaze upon the sparkling gem which adorned it, smiled, and murmured: "How surprised he will be—how surprised they will *all* be! And I have not told auntie yet, but I must, this very day. I must talk with Poke, too, and ascertain if he desires to go back to his old home."

According to these resolutions, that same evening after supper, seated in the shielding twilight, she took Mr. and Mrs. Hosmar into her confidence, told of her "engagement," and informed them *who* "Mr. Clark" was.

"Wal, ef that don't beat all!" exclaimed Mrs. Hosmar. "To think of your comin' away out here, to git red of his father's persecutions on his account, an' now! Wal, wal! What *is* to be *will* be, an' thar's no use fightin' ag'in' it!"

"That may be so, Rachel; but it's my opinion that if she'd a-stayed at home, an' he'd a-come thar, she'd a-hated him like pizen! So thar wa'n't no harm done by her comin' 'long with us. I b'lieve he's a first-rate feller, an' uncommon smart too, an' I'm glad everything's turned out jest as it has!"

"I'm much obliged to you, uncle Hosmar, for your good opinion of him; but what do you think he will say when he finds my name is no more 'Hosmar' than his was 'Clark'?"

"Ha! Ha! Turn about is fair play! But no one said your name *was* Hosmar; they all took it fur granted. I reckon, tho', we all called you Annie, an' said nothin' about the rest of it!"

"I shall start for home in two or three weeks. Have you any objections to my taking Poke with me?"

"Why, ef he wants to go, you might as well take him, I reckon. I allowed to have him help me farm this summer, but ef he gits homesick an' stubborn, he wouldn't amount to much nohow!"

"Well, then, I will see him about it in the morning, and you may mention and explain my going away to the Bokers. I could never endure the questioning and 'wonderment' of the good folks, to tell them myself. But, keep the rest of my affairs unmentioned until after I am gone, if you please; then you may tell them all about it."

"Ef you are a-goin' away so soon, you'll leave us right smart in your debt. You paid us fur a year's board, you know, an'—"

"Mr. Hosmar—aunt Rachel, unless you *wish* to offend me you will never mention that matter again. I have, ever since I can remember, received care and kindness which *no* money could have bought, and none can repay. I shall always be your debtor."

The next day the subject of returning to Kentucky was broached to Poke, who expressed himself willing and anxious to see the old home again.

"Dar ain't any colored folks here any whar's round, an' w'en you is gone, Miss Annie, dar won't be anybody dat I has any feelin's fur. Massa Hosmar's a mighty clever man, an' I t'ink a heap of 'em all, but den dey isn't *our kind of folks,* you know!"

"*Our* kind of folks," was delivered with an air of importance, as if the best blood of the land flowed in his veins; and perhaps some of it did! Annie smiled, and replied: "I was in hopes that you *would* like the West, get yourself a home and some land; but if you do not, it will be best for you not to stay. I have a plan for you, however, which I think you *will* like. You know the little place just out of town, which old Mr. Brown lived upon for so many years? Well, the old man is dead—Mrs. Plyne wrote to me about it—and his wife has gone to live with one of her married children. The cottage is empty; there are ten acres of land, and I think with that, and your trade, you can earn a good deal of money. I will hire Melissy's time for a year or two and let her keep house for you; she is an excellent laundress and can be of service to me, as well as earn a good many dollars working for other families, and I think, with the amount of money you already have laid up, you can, both together, soon earn her freedom! Eight hundred dollars will buy her, I suppose, and that by close economy you both can save in two years."

"Oh, Miss Annie! You're jest like yer blessed mother, an' she was an angel 'fore she went to heaben!" cried the delighted man, with tears rolling down his cheeks.

"Oh no, Poke. I never can be half what dear mamma was, but I will always do what I can for her old favorite!" and Annie turned away to seek her own room, her own eyes full of tears, as this mention of her dearly loved mother brought her vividly to mind.

In about two weeks from the time last mentioned, Annie's preparations for leaving her western home were completed. A light spring-wagon had been hired at Blufftown, and Mr. Hosmar was to accompany her to Council Bluffs, see her safely *en route* to St. Joseph's, where she expected to find a boat for St. Louis, and return the wagon to the proprietor. The morning fixed upon for her departure was as pleasant as it was possible for a bright, spring morning to be.

Squire Boker and his wife, and Mary, came over to see her off, and to say good-by.

"I tell ye what," said the squire. "We hate most powerful bad to see ye go! We thought an awful sight of Clark, but I don't know but what you've cut him out, fur neither Molly nur me cried when *he* went away, an' I b'lieve *she's* a-cryin' now, an' I feel ez if I wus a-goin' to blubber!"

"I shall always remember my kind friends here on the prairie; and I hope to see you all again *sometime;* so you must not forget me. I have left a few keepsakes for you, Molly, to 'remember me by.' Auntie will give them to you after I am gone."

"It don't seem to me one bit ez if you wus a great heiress an' one of the 'big-bugs' I've heerd so much about, you've allers been so friendly and clever with us!" exclaimed Mrs. Boker.

"I am just what I am, rich or poor, Mrs. Boker; and I prize a good, kind friend when I find one; but Mr. Hosmar is ready, I believe; so good-by all—you last, dear auntie! I will write to you when I reach home. Good-by! Good-by!"

The wagon rolled away, and left a tearful group watching it. The squire took out his yellow cotton-handkerchief and blew a sounding blast.

"Thar's no use a-talkin', but that gal is one of a thousand, an' we won't never see another one like her!" He sighed deeply as he spoke.

CHAPTER NINE

A SNAG, AND WHERE IS HE?

Annie Howard stood upon the deck of the river-boat *Hesperian,* leaning upon the railing, and watching for those pleasant bits of scenery which she, every now and then, glided into along the shore.

The spring rains, and the melting of the mountain snows, had swollen the Missouri into a mighty flood, and she noticed that, ever and anon, as the steamer swept along, it received into its waves great slices of earth which often were covered with a growth of large trees, and other vegetation. Presently two or three ladies from the cabin came out upon the deck and joined her in watching the river and the shore; soon after they did so the steamer's whistle sounded a signal which arrested their attention and caused them to glance around, and from one side of the river to the other, in expectation of seeing a town or at least a group of passengers on the bank waiting to be taken aboard.

"The boat is going to stop; but I can't discover even the vestige of a city, village, steamboat-landing or stray passenger!" exclaimed one of the ladies.

"I see a big pile of wood just ahead," said Annie. "They are going to take on fuel."

Just then the boat turned toward the shore, and as she swung around there was a shock, a sudden confusion on the lower deck, a Babel of voices and sounds which caused the terrified ladies to rush into the cabin in search of friends and information.

The boat, in rounding-to, had struck a snag with such force as nearly to break her in two.

Fortunately there were but few passengers aboard, and by the prompt measures and entire self-possession of the officers of the *Hesperian,* all were safely landed on the shore, before she filled and sunk.

"Thank goodness, Miss Annie, you is safe, sure 'nuff. Cap'in wouldn't gib me no time to look 'round; jess shuffled me inter de boat head furs'!" exclaimed Poke, as he made his way to Annie, where she sat upon a log of wood, in company with several companions in distress.

"Yes, Poke, I'm safe, so far, and I'm glad to see that you are, too," replied Annie, with rather a wan smile.

"Dear me! *Isn't* this a dismal place!" sighed one of the ladies, disconsolately.

"Mr. Smith, come here, do!" called another to her husband, who was assisting the officers to rescue some baggage that had been cast adrift from the wreck. "What are we to do—sit on this wood-pile all night, with a chance of being 'dumped' into the river before morning?"

"Not *quite* so bad as that, wife! The captain says that there is a shanty about half a mile back in the woods, which will furnish a tolerably comfortable shelter for you ladies until morning, when the *Arrow* will be coming down and will take us on."

"What an idea! We'd be afraid, alone in the woods; and besides that, how are we to get there? My feet and clothes are wet, and I have no bonnet or shawl. Oh, dear!" and the poor woman began to cry.

"Afraid! Why your brother Ben and myself and the captain and half a dozen more will escort you there, and see you safely established; then we will build a roaring fire near at hand and camp around it, so that neither musketoes, wild animals, nor wild Missourians will dare disturb you."

"Indeed, ladies," said the captain. "I don't know of any thing better to do. The *Arrow* won't be down before ten o'clock to-morrow. The cabin referred to belongs to some men who have been chopping wood for our line, and they have cleared out a very good road through the timber, they say, so that the walking will not be difficult."

"Well, any thing by way of adventure," cried Mrs. Smith, beginning to recover her usual cheerfulness. "I hope the gentlemen of the house will receive us with genuine Western hospitality, and get up some entertainment worthy of the occasion!"

"The 'gentlemen of the house' propose to resign matters altogether into your own hands, ladies—they are here in the crowd somewheres now, and I think you would be quite willing to dispense with their attentions if you should chance to see them; they look like 'hard cases,'" replied the captain, laughing.

At this moment a tall, roughly-dressed fellow crowded up and peered over the shoulders of those nearest the group of ladies. As he did so Annie glanced toward him, and instantly recognized Mr. Hosmar's old foe, Bill Larkins. She involuntarily sprung to her feet with a little exclamation of surprise, which at once attracted the fellow's attention, and caused him to send a swift and startled glance throughout the crowd as though to discover who might be with her; then, with an air of unconcern, he sauntered away among the crowd until he was convinced that she was unaccompanied by any of her friends. Thus reassured, with an impudent swagger he approached her, and remarked in a low, sneering tone:

"Seems to me you hev a pecoolier faculty fur gittin' inter scrapes, young woman."

Annie did not reply, but motioned to Poke, who stood at a little distance, to come to her. As he approached, Larkins surveyed him deliberately from head to foot, and then, placing his great hand roughly upon Poke's shoulder, resumed:

"So this nigger belongs to *you,* does he, Miss Hosmar? A likely lookin' feller, too."

Poke shook off the hand indignantly, and Annie remarked quietly:

"You would do well, Mr. Larkins, to leave me and my 'nigger' to ourselves. I have no desire whatever to converse with you."

"Oh, wal, jest as you please 'bout that; thought mebbe you'd be glad to see me. S'pose you'll pay a visit to my cabin tho', an' be glad of the chance," and he turned away with an insulting laugh.

"I wish you'd reques' me, Miss Annie, to knock dat low-live trash down!" exclaimed Poke, fairly swelling with indignation.

"No indeed, Poke. Keep altogether away from him, and stay as near me as you can until we are on the river again."

It was now almost sundown, and the gloom of evening was beginning to settle down upon the woods. Clouds were gathering in the west, and a chilling wind swept across the water. The gentlemen who were to escort the ladies to the shelter of the cabin, now urged haste, that all their preparations for passing the night might be completed before dark.

When the party was about ready to start, Mrs. Smith approached Annie, with her brother Ben, and said:

"Miss Howard, this is my brother, Mr. Tisdale; he would be pleased to act as your escort through the woods, or serve you in any way you may desire."

"I am very much obliged to Mr. Tisdale, and to yourself, too, Mrs. Smith. I was beginning to feel quite forlorn," replied Annie, with a frank smile, and accepting at once the offered arm. The whole party now set out upon their walk, making merry of their mishaps and rather doleful plight.

When the cabin was reached, it was found to contain a cooking-stove, a rough bench, table, and bed, and was tolerably clean. So with much merriment the party began their preparations for passing the night there.

The captain announced that provisions enough had been rescued from the wreck to furnish a comfortable supper and breakfast, and the cook, with the convenience of the cooking-stove and tea kettle belonging to the establishment, would soon have ready a refreshing cup o' tea.

Soon an immense fire was roaring out under the stars, and a picturesque group surrounding it. The ladies, attracted by the cheerful gleams of the blazing heap, had deserted the shanty, and were accommodated to seats upon a huge, mossy log, which had been rolled up to the fire for that purpose.

Song-singing, and a number of merry games, filled up the hours of the early evening, till Annie suddenly exclaimed:

"I wonder where Poke is! Have you seen him this evening, Mr. Tisdale?"

"Not for an hour or two, I'm certain, Miss Howard. Do you want him?"

"I want to know where he is. I charged him not to leave me; I must find him at once."

But, although Poke was called and searched for, he could not be found.

The cook and one of the waiters belonging to the boat, having just come up from the river, were questioned, but they declared that they had seen nothing of him since he left the landing with the rest of the party.

After an hour of waiting and anxiety, while a search was going on, Annie sat down upon the log before the fire to think. The gentlemen gathered around, one suggesting one thing and one another, when Mr. Smith exclaimed:

"I'm willing to bet all creation that these rascally Missourian wood-choppers have got hold of him!"

"I have been thinking of that, too," said Annie "What can be done?"

"Pretty considerable of a loss—worth a thousand dollars or more!" resumed Mr. Smith, indignantly.

"'Tis not that! 'Tis not that!" began Annie, when a voice near her caused her to start to her feet and look behind her. Just back of the log, in the shadow of a tree, stood Bill Larkins, regarding her with a gratified grin.

"Lost yer nigger, hev ye, miss? Wal, thar's allers nigger stealers round these steamboat landin's; but, mebbe he went off on his own hook—hey?"

"He *may* have done that, certainly; I had not thought of *that* probability—" began Mr. Smith, but Annie interrupted him.

"No, indeed!" she exclaimed. "He has been foully dealt with in *some* way, and I am perfectly sure that this man here knows where he is!" But when they glanced again to where Larkins had stood, he was gone; and although they searched the woods perserveringly, they saw him no more that night.

"Why do you suspect this man so strongly, Miss Howard?" inquired Mr. Tisdale, as the party gathered around the fire again.

Annie then related what she knew of his character, and told to an interested audience the story of the claim-fight and the burnt cabin. When Squire Boker's name was mentioned, Mr. Tisdale exclaimed:

"I am well acquainted with the squire—I was one of a party of returned Californians who camped near his house for several weeks. We thought him quite a 'character,' and liked him heartily."

"Yes, I have often heard him tell the story. He had one of your number still with him when we went there," said Annie.

"What! Charlie Norris still in the West? What in the world— Well, to hear that you know Charlie and the squire makes me feel as though you, too, were an old acquaintance and friend. And so this Larkins is the scoundrel who took possession of your uncle's land? Well, I begin to think that he *has* captured that poor fellow, and means to make a speculation out of him."

"I feel certain of it," answered Annie. "What can be done?"

"I hardly know. This is the very place of all others for the perpetration of such a deed. The captain has gone down to the river to make inquiries, and if, when he comes back, nothing has been ascertained about him, we will 'hold a consultation,' as the doctors say, and see what is best to be done. Meanwhile we will replenish the fire, and some one shall tell a story to make the time seem short."

"That is a capital suggestion, Ben," exclaimed Mrs. Smith. "And you are the very one to tell it."

"I!" exclaimed Tisdale, with an air of consternation.

"Yes, you! You!" resounded from all sides.

"If I had known what my suggestion would lead to, I should not have made it!"

"Yes, but you *have* made it, so begin, 'Once upon a time,'" remarked one of the ladies.

"Well, then: 'Once upon a time,' when I was young and inexperienced—"

"*Ages* and *ages* ago," whispered Mrs. Smith, in a loud "aside" to Annie.

"—When I was young and inexperienced," repeated Mr. Tisdale, "I started out to seek my fortune. It was generally supposed in those days that fortunes were to be found ready-made in California; therefore I turned my credulous steps that way. My expectations and anticipations were all *couleur de rose,* and when I found myself upon the golden shores, I began at once to look around for 'nuggets.' If I chanced to strike my foot against a stone, I was sure to look down to see if any thing of importance had turned up.

"But, before very long, that kind of feeling wore off, and I joined a company of five men, who were fitting out for a newly-discovered diggings.

"They were a rough set of men, but seemed honest and good-natured, and I expected to be greatly benefited by their larger experience in the business, which was to be set off against the pleasure they would receive from my society!

"We agreed among ourselves that as long as we worked together we would 'share and share alike,' and at the close of each day's operations, would divide the gain equally among us.

"After we arrived at the diggings and began work, I seemed to be specially favored with good 'luck.' Scarcely a day but something unusual came in my way, so that when we came together to count our gains and divide them, I was almost certain to have something above the average to show. For a time the men seemed pleased, and called me their 'lucky partner,' and appeared to think themselves fortunate in having such a clever fellow among their number; but after a while they began to display feelings of jealousy and dislike toward me, and seemed to suspect that I was secreting a part of my gains, and did not throw into the common stock all that I found. This made me indignant, and I determined to leave them and strike out for myself.

"I had noticed, not more than half a mile from our camp, a little rocky ravine, through which a tiny brook trickled, which I knew must, at some seasons of the year, swell into a considerable torrent. It struck me that, amid the crevices of the rocks over which the stream dashed when swollen, there might be deposits worth looking for. So, after a formal 'dissolving of partnership,' I started off with my 'pick' upon my shoulder, and my knapsack of provisions on my back, and taking a course calculated to mislead my whilom partners if they should be disposed to watch me, I eventually made my way to the place.

"The very first day—mark how fortune favors the brave—I found amid the sand and *debris* which filled a fissure in the rocks, a number of shining particles, which elated me to such a degree that I performed untellable wonders in the way of rending rocks asunder, and getting at places that seemed inaccessible. To be brief, I found so much of the precious stuff that I determined to make a permanent camp in a sort of hidden nook which I had discovered further up the ravine, lay in a stock of provisions, and go to work in earnest.

"In about a week I was fully established, and had gold enough to make me think I was almost rich. But one night I awakened suddenly from deep sleep, with a feeling of danger which I could not shake off.

The night was dark, and the depth of the ravine made it profoundly so, and I strained my eyes in vain to pierce the darkness.

"For a few moments I lay perfectly still, until I was certain that I heard whispering voices and stealthy feet. Then I rose as silently as possible, and grasping my revolver, waited to see what was to happen. Presently a sudden stream of light was thrown forward into the nook where I stood, and revealed my position to the intruders, while, at the same time, I caught a glimpse of them. There were two or three men, I am not certain which, for as soon as they saw me the light was extinguished and three or four shots were fired in my direction. I fired in return, and then instantly changed my position; another volley came, and a ball struck my revolver from my hand. I sprung forward to recover it, and while I was groping around for it, I received a blow upon my head which rendered me senseless.

"What immediately followed—I of course do not know, but I *do* know that the scoundrels bound me hand and foot, discovered my hoarded treasure and carried it away with them, leaving me, in the fond expectation, I suppose, that if I recovered from my blow upon my head, I would perish with hunger and thirst.

"When I recovered consciousness, it was early morning; my senses were so confused, and my brain so dizzy that 'twas an hour or two before I could collect strength enough to try to loosen my bonds; and when I *did* try, I found myself powerless. I struggled and fumed until completely exhausted, when I fell into a sort of stupor which must have ended in fever and delirium.

"When I again opened my eyes to the realities of life, I found myself lying in a small tent, upon a comfortable bed of dried grass and blankets, and bending over me was a kind, compassionate face, with tender blue eyes, and a little brown hand was bathing my head with cold water. I closed my eyes again with a vague feeling of uncertainty as to my own identity, and when I opened them once more, another face—that of an old man with white hair and a pleasant countenance—was bending beside the first.

"It took me some time to 'take in' and comprehend my condition and surroundings, but when I did so, I found that the tender, blue-eyed face belonged to a youth apparently about sixteen years old who answered to the name of 'Jamie,' and addressed the elderly person as 'father.'

"The old man told me presently that, while passing near the ravine about sundown the evening before on his way home from a 'station' where he had been to procure provisions, he heard a groan as of some one in distress, and after a little search had found me, and with the aid of his mule had succeeded in getting me to his tent, about three miles further on; and that since, he and Jamie had done all that their limited resources would allow them to do, for my comfort and recovery.

"There was something peculiarly fascinating and attractive about Jamie. His brown hair curled in close, soft rings all over his head, and although his face was very brown, 'twas refined and pretty—yes, pretty! There was nothing masculine about it except the faint flush of an incipient mustache; he wore a frock of common blue cotton stuff, gathered in at the waist by a black leather belt, and reaching about half-way to his knees; his father wore one of the same kind and each belt held a revolver.

"Lying there, part of the time dozing stupidly, part of the time acutely conscious of every tone and motion, it was not two days before I was fully persuaded in my own mind that my young friend was a girl.

"And, to cut my story short, I found that my surmise was correct; that Jamie was, aforetime, Jennie; that she was her father's only child; that she had lost her mother years before; that when her father had determined to seek his fortunes in the fabled land of gold, she made up her mind to accompany him, and would not be dissuaded, and to avoid remark and annoyance in that womanless land, had adopted the masculine costume; that the mustache was burnt cork; that they had been tolerably successful and were soon going back to the states—and—and—"

"*And that*," said Mrs. Smith, maliciously taking up the theme at this interesting point, "Jennie was a perfect little witch—*and* that her father, after leaving California, bought up ever so many sections of land in Iowa, *and* has founded a young city—*and* brother Ben has been out to locate—*and* has persuaded Mr. Smith and myself that 'tis to *our* interest to settle out West too—*AND* there is to be a wedding the first of June if nothing 'happens to hinder.' "

Another half-hour passed before the captain made his appearance.

Poke had not been seen by any one at the landing since he left it in company with his mistress. "And," added the captain, "I am sorry to say that there is more bad news to tell. We will have to break camp here and get back to the bluffs immediately. The river is rising like all possessed, and there's no telling where it will be by morning."

"Thunderation!" exclaimed Mr. Smith; and "Oh, dear!" cried all the ladies.

"How can the river be rising?" asked Annie. "There has been no rain recently."

"The melting of the snows in the mountains, madam; the weather has been unusually warm for this season of the year, and there has been heavy rains in the back country, too, I think, and so we are likely to have our 'June freshet' in April."

"Considerable baggage was taken off the boat, was there not, captain?" asked Tisdale.

"Yes; the men are bringing up every thing portable that they can carry through the woods. They have pressed the wood-choppers' team and lumber-wagon into service, and what can not be brought away now will be swallowed up by the 'big muddy' before morning."

"Pray let *us* get away before we are swallowed up too!" exclaimed Mrs. Smith, excitedly.

"How far will we be obliged to go?" asked Tisdale.

"About half a mile. There is a little town called Jacksonville, just beyond this bottom-land."

" 'Tis an ill wind that blows nobody good," remarked Mr. Tisdale to Annie, as he offered her his arm for the walk to Jacksonville. "This delay will give us time and opportunity to search for your missing man."

CHAPTER TEN

THE ROMANCE OF
SETTLEMENT LIFE

Every little town has its "hotel," and the *Stranger's Home,* of Jacksonville, was a fair sample of its class. It was dirty, ill-kept, tumble-down, and dismal in every respect; and when, in addition to the fatigue, excitement, and anxiety of the previous night, Annie found herself, after a few hours of restless sleep, standing alone, gazing through the dim and smoky windows of the sitting-room, upon floods of driving, whirling rain which drenched and beat upon the few scattered and dilapidated houses that comprised "Jacksonville," she felt her spirits sinking in unwonted depression.

But presently the cheerful voice of the lively Mrs. Smith, and the entrance of several of the party, who had but just emerged from their respective apartments, roused her from the despondency into which she had fallen.

"Good-morning, Miss Howard. You are admiring the prospect, I suppose," was Mr. Tisdale's salutation as he entered the room.

"To tell the truth, Mr. Tisdale, I was indulging in some rather unpleasant reflections!" responded Annie.

"Well!" exclaimed Mrs. Smith. "I felt so *dreadfully* 'blue' this morning that I couldn't endure it at all. So I quarreled with Mr. Smith, scolded Ben, and upbraided the captain for our misfortune, and now I really feel much better."

Annie laughed, and Tisdale remarked in an aside to her:

"If 'twould afford *you* any relief to have some one to scold or quarrel with, I'm at your service."

"Thank you," answered Annie. "But I will try to be content with abusing the weather. I never before saw it rain as it does this morning."

"It has been raining just so for hours; our last night's camp is under water before this time."

"And we can't get away from this abominable place while it continues—that's the worst of it!" grumbled Mr. Smith.

"Have you made any inquiries yet concerning Mr. Larkins or Poke?" asked Annie.

"Yes, I have found out that this Larkins lives three or four miles further back in the country, and that the man who has been helping him chop wood for the boats is a brother-in-law and lives with him. They are considered decidedly 'hard cases.' The landlord says that they have only been engaged in the woods here for a few weeks, and have been strongly suspected of horse-stealing and other nefarious business. 'Twould be an easy matter to get up a party to hunt for him, and rescue the man, if he is in his hands, if it were not for this storm."

"I think there is every prospect of a second deluge," remarked Mr. Smith, discontentedly.

And, indeed, as the day advanced, the storm grew really terrific. Peal after peal of thunder crashed through the air, and the lightning flashed with an intensity actually appalling, while floods of water dashed down upon the earth, and were whirled about by the wind, which roared and shrieked and howled as though a demon himself was battling with the other elements.

Thus the storm raged all through that day and the succeeding night, but on the morning of the second day, an unclouded sun, a calm blue sky, and a soft spring wind reigned over the earth once more.

The travelers were eager to be again upon their way, but the captain, the landlord, and the other authorities declared that the streams between Jacksonville and the next town where there was a good landing for boats, would be swollen and bridgeless, and utterly impassable for another day at least; so, with much discontent, they sought to resign themselves to their fate.

About an hour after breakfast, while a party headed by Tisdale and the landlord were about ready to start upon their expedition to the suspected squatter's cabin, an excited crowd of men and boys were seen hurrying down the street, and the cause of the commotion soon appeared. As some of the village boys were paddling about in an old canoe, on the river-bottom, that morning, they had discovered, entangled among some bushes and low trees in the water, the body of a man, whether white or black they had not stayed to see, but, terrified half out of their senses, had hastened back to the village, and reported what they had seen.

Tisdale concluded, almost instantly, that the drowned man was Poke, and thought it best to relate the circumstance of the finding of the body, and his conjectures on the subject, to Annie, without delay. He accordingly returned to the house, and communicated what he had heard to the ladies in the sitting-room, who had been watching the crowd in the street with great curiosity. To Annie he said:

"It *may* be that Poke, in strolling into the woods that night, became bewildered and lost in the darkness, and was overtaken by the overflowing waters, and drowned. I hope not, indeed, and I will go at once and see for myself, and report as soon as possible." And the young man hastened away and joined the crowd which was hurrying forward toward the point of interest.

Annie felt that there was, indeed, a probability that Poke's disappearance might thus be accounted for, and she reproached herself bitterly for having been instrumental in bringing him into danger. Tears filled her eyes, too, when she remembered how devoted and faithful he had always been to herself, and with what affection her mother had regarded him—remembering and providing for his welfare in her dying hours.

Slowly the moments passed; she wished, yet dreaded, to hear tidings; and thus, with a sad heart, she sat at a window watching the deserted street.

A cloud seemed to rest upon the spirits of all, for there is that in a sudden or mysterious death which impresses the soul with awe and dread.

Two or three hours passed before the villagers returned, and then they came carrying in their midst a rude bier, upon which lay a human form. Annie shuddered and turned away from the window before the crowd reached the street; but in another moment Mr. Tisdale entered the room, and approaching her, said:

"Our fears in this case, Miss Howard, were unfounded. The body found is not that of your servant, but of his supposed abductor!"

"The unhappy wretch!" cried Annie, horrified at such a termination of so evil a life. Then for a moment her countenance lighted up, and she gave a sigh of relief.

"But," continued Mr. Tisdale, "there is reason to fear that Poke has met with a similar fate. There is no doubt but that Larkins had him in hiding, in the woods near the river. In fact, I am quite certain of it. Do you know this handkerchief?"

"Certainly, I do!" cried Annie, taking the large silk handkerchief which Tisdale offered for her inspection. "I gave this to Poke, and embroidered this little device on the white myself!"

"Well, I found it tied around the dead man's throat, and remembered it at once. Poke was very fond of displaying it, and I had noticed it several times in his possession, and laughed at the poor fellow's evident desire to exhibit its beauties."

"And you think——" began Annie, in a questioning tone.

"I think," resumed Tisdale, "that Larkins was hiding in the woods, and had Poke secreted near the river, expecting to run him off into the interior of the State after we were out of the way, and that he either left him to his fate when he found himself in peril, or that, in attempting to take him out, they both blundered into the slough near which this body was found, and while the bushes caught and held this one, the other might have sunk out of sight or floated away."

"Oh, if I only knew!" cried Annie. "There is a possibility that he escaped; uncertainty is so hard to bear!"

"Well, I have engaged half a dozen young fellows to explore the river-bottom, and they are paddling about now in every direction. I do not know of any thing else that I can do in the matter, excepting to go out to where this man's family lives, and *that* I will do this afternoon. I have engaged a horse for that purpose, and our landlord will accompany me, to carry the tidings of misfortune."

The body of the dead squatter was deposited in the barroom of the Stranger's Home, and an idle crowd lingered about to discuss the matter, and regale themselves with gossip and whisky.

Seldom was their little village distinguished by such a succession of remarkable events. There had been, within forty hours, the wrecking of the steamboat, the arrival of an unprecedented number of guests at the "hotel," an extraordinary storm, and the finding of a drowned man!

But they were destined to still another sensation, for, a little after noon, a rumor of the most exciting character flew through the village, and diverted the attention of all from the discussion of the late accident, and directed it into quite another channel.

The boys employed by Mr. Tisdale to explore the woods had returned to town in great haste and trepidation, reporting that they had seen an enormous black bear in a tree about half-way between the bluffs and the river!

Great was the hilarity which now prevailed. A bear-hunt was becoming a rarity in those parts, and was just the thing to finish up appropriately an idle day, and dispel the melancholy feelings engendered by the morning's discovery.

Guns were hastily hunted up, and the little grocery-keeper on the corner was nearly overwhelmed with demands for powder and lead. Half-a-dozen small rafts were speedily constructed and "manned," while numbers of adventurous spirits started forth, each upon a single board, and with a pole in hand to steer with.

"If the old feller takes to the water we'll see fun; he'd play hob with these rafts," cried one of the men, jocosely.

"We'll play hob with *him* if we once git a good sight on him," replied another.

"The feller that brings him down gits the hide!" exclaimed a third.

And thus, amid much excitement and hilarity, the hunters got started, and began to work their way among the trees in the direction pointed out to them by the boys who had discovered the animal.

As they advanced further into the woods they grew more silent, not wishing to alarm the bear and give him a chance to escape. Some of the men kept a lookout, while others steered the way among the trees. After proceeding thus for half-a-mile, one of the men announced that he saw the animal in a large tree at a considerable distance further toward the southwest than their present course would lead to. The fleet immediately came to a stop, while all eagerly peered through the swaying tree-tops which intercepted the view.

A half-suppressed shout rose, as, far up amid the branches of an immense cottonwood, the object of the hunt was seen. Guns were cocked, and the party again moved forward, every man not engaged in managing the rafts keeping his eye fixed in an eager gaze in the direction indicated, while a plan of attack was discussed in vehement though subdued tones.

"I'll be dogged if I don't think this is goin' to be ruther a ticklish business," remarked one tall fellow, looking very much as though he wished himself somewhere else, " 'cause if the varmint takes to the water and gits in among us, thar'll be some on us upsot, that's certain!"

"If you're *afeered* you kin take this canoe and paddle back home; but if you *do*, don't expect to be invited to the barbecue to-night!" exclaimed a young man, in a sarcastic tone.

"Who's a-talkin' about backin' out?" retorted the first speaker, angrily. "Mibbe you'll be the first one to git a duckin' yerself."

"If I am, I kin stand it," was the scornful reply.

"Now, boys, shut up yer quarrelin', an watch out fur the game. Here's the slough, an' we kin hev a clearer look-out, and easier paddling!"

A few moments after, one of the men remarked:

"Well, if I ain't awfully mistaken, that thing over thar ain't no bear."

"What is it?" cried half a dozen voices.

"Looks more like a man, to me."

"I'll be durned if it ain't."

"What in thunder's the matter?" called out someone from the rear.

"Why, our *bear* has turned into a *man!*"

"Move on—move on, and let us see."

And, as the party approached nearer, they plainly saw the figure of a man crouching among the branches high overhead.

"It's a nigger. Some cussed runaway, as like as not. Mebbe 'twon't be such a bad haul, after all!" cried the foremost man.

"I expect it's the one that young gent at the tavern was inquirin' about," answered another.

"That's the kink. Let's make him fork over handsome fer finding him," said the faint-hearted fellow who thought bear-hunting ticklish business.

"Shove up, boys. If he's been treed here ever sence the water riz, he must be purty nigh tuckered out."

It was, indeed, poor Poke, so exhausted and bewildered by terror, fasting, and exposure, that it was with much difficulty that the men succeeded in getting him down from his lofty perch. His limbs were so cramped and stiffened by the constrained position in which he had remained for such a length of time, that they were almost useless.

He seemed to regard every one around him as a foe, and could not be made to answer one of the questions addressed to him.

"I reckon he's clear gin out. Hain't none of ye got a bottle of whisky along, so's to give him a leetle?" remarked one of the men.

Half a dozen flasks were instantly produced, and Poke urged to drink; but he seemed deaf, dumb, and blind, until finally a few drops were literally poured into his mouth.

The expedition then prepared to return to Jacksonville, and it must be acknowledged that it presented rather a crestfallen appearance as it neared the bluffs and met the expectant crowd anxiously awaiting them to view the trophy of the hunt.

Poke, who either could not or would not help himself in the least, was lifted into an old cart near at hand, which the boys of the crowd pushed and pulled along until they reached the Stranger's Home. He was then carried into the house, and laid upon the bar-room lounge, and a messenger was dispatched to the parlor to say that a darky had been found in the woods, and requesting the travelers to come and see if he was the man missing from their company. Those interested hastened into the bar-room, and Annie eagerly advanced toward the lounge.

"It *is* he—poor fellow! Where did you find him?"

Poke, who had lain motionless and with closed eyes ever since he had been brought in, now started up into a sitting position, and cried, with a trembling voice:

"Is dat *you,* Miss Annie!" and instantly fell back in a swoon.

Restoratives were given, and some nourishing food prepared and administered in small quantities, until the famished and exhausted creature recovered strength enough to relate the story of his misfortunes, which was substantially as follows:

Feeling sleepy and tired on the evening of the disaster on the river, he had, while the party were all gathered around the camp-fire, seated himself in the doorway of the cabin, and fallen asleep.

He was awakened by being raised to his feet, and found himself with his hands tied behind him, and a large handkerchief drawn tightly over his mouth. Larkins stood by him, grasping his arm with one powerful hand, while he displayed a pistol with the other; and as soon as Poke was sufficiently awake to comprehend his situation, he whispered into his ear:

"Now march right straight along with me, without attemptin' to make any noise whatever. Do as yer told, or I'll put half a dozen bullets through yer thick skull afore ye kin wink!"

Thus he forced him through the woods for half a mile, perhaps, when he stopped and tied his captive securely to a tree, and there left him to himself for an hour or two, nearly frantic with despair and terror.

It was at this time, doubtless, that Larkins had shown himself at the camp, though for what purpose does not clearly appear.

He then returned to his prisoner, took him some distance further into the woods, and again tied him to a tree, around which grew a tangle of brush and weeds, which formed a very good hiding place, and, after fastening him so securely that 'twould be an impossibility for him to free himself, he left him, saying that after the boat passed down the river in the morning, and his mistress and friends were out of the way, he would return and take him on further.

The air was chilly and damp, and in the after part of the night it began to rain. Before morning the storm was raging furiously, and poor Poke found the water rising around him until it reached his knees. In vain were all his frantic efforts to release himself, and he at length gave himself up as utterly lost, when he found himself roughly grasped, and his bonds hastily unfastened by his abductor, who ordered him to instantly climb into a tree.

"I was awfully afraid that you'd be a gone-up nigger before I could git to ye! It got infernally dark 'long toward morning that I couldn't venture a step, and I like to never have got here. Git yerself up thar; we'll hev to roost here till this rain's over, and don't ye attempt to come down till I give the word. Thar ain't no sort of a chance of you gittin' away from *me*. If ye feel like tryin' it, jist remember that I'm close by, a-watching ye with this little weapon handy! Thar'll be a feller along after a while with a boat, an' we'll take a nice little ride an' visit some partic'lar friends of mine up the river!"

Poke climbed into the tree in which he was finally discovered, and Larkins into another near by.

When the terrific storm of lightning, wind, and rain came on, it was almost impossible to keep himself from being torn from his position and dashed down into the water beneath him.

During a lull in the storm, Larkins shouted across to him:

"The devil's got every one of them folks that camped down by the river last night! Ye could swim a steamboat now whar that shanty stood!"

Poor Poke was only too certain that the last assertion might be true, and what little hope and courage there was left in him gave way, leaving only a sense of the deepest despair.

A few moments after this, a blinding flash of lightning caused him to shut his eyes in dread, and a crash of thunder seemed to shake the whole earth; and when he again opened his eyes and looked around, he saw that the tree in which Larkins had stationed himself was shivered into splinters, and that the miserable man who but just before had spoken to him, was floating in the water at some distance away!

Poke could not remember with any distinctness how the time intervening between that awful event, and his rescue by the bear-hunters, passed. He lost all sensation of hunger and thirst, and felt altogether indifferent to his own safety. He thought that "Miss Annie" was drowned, and when he heard her voice after being taken to the village tavern, he was so surprised and delighted that, in his weak and exhausted state, he fell into a swoon.

When young Tisdale and the landlord returned from their expedition into the back country, they had also a tale of horror to tell.

Upon reaching the suspected squatter's cabin, they found it unroofed and nearly demolished by the storm, while within, among the ruins, lay, unwatched and unguarded, the bruised and soulless body of the squatter's wife!

The same avenging bolt may have ended both their wretched lives. The brother-in-law and partner was nowhere to be found, and was never again seen in that vicinity. Perhaps the waters of the mighty Missouri held the secret of his disappearance.

"This has been a day of horrors! I hope to-morrow may see us on our way—I shall never want to think of this place again!" exclaimed Mr. Tisdale, as the whole party of travelers were gathered in the parlor in the evening.

"*I* shan't get over it for six months, I know!" remarked his sister, dolefully.

"I have engaged conveyances to take us all over to Longport in the morning, and 'twill be the day for the *Queen of the West* to be down. I prophesy that we'll all take tea in St. Louis to-morrow evening!"

"So mote it be!" cried Mr. Smith, energetically.

––––––––––

The next morning proved a delightful one; nothing happened to hinder the impatient travelers, but, after a pleasant and exhilarating ride over the prairie, they reached Longport, an hour ahead of the "*Queen's*" time, so that Mrs. Smith was enabled to procure a new bonnet, and the other ladies of the party to repair, somewhat, the damage sustained by their traveling costumes.

On the evening of the same day they reached, without further mishap, the city of St. Louis, and Annie was received into the conciliating embraces of her anxious and expectant friends who were to meet her there.

CHAPTER ELEVEN

IT IS WELL!

"How glad I am that you are at home again, Annie. Father seems cheered up wonderfully, though he is very feeble; don't you think so?"

"He *does* seem to have failed in health very much since last fall. Has your brother been to see him?"

Mrs. Plyne was surprised that Annie should mention what she supposed must be a disagreeable subject to her, but she hastily replied:

"No, not yet. He has been in California for some time, and only returned to the States a few weeks ago. I had a letter from him just after his arrival in Thurston—the first one we have received for months. It contained important news too—he is to be married some time this summer, he says, so, if he *should* make us a visit you need not fear any 'further persecutions' on his account!"

"I am glad to hear it!" said Annie, looking down steadily at the little ring upon her finger, and twirling it around with energy. "And I think that, under the circumstances, it would be well to write and urge him to make his father a visit; his coming might have a beneficial effect upon papa's health and spirits."

'Twas very seldom that Annie had called Mr. Norris "papa," but the habit of doing so seemed to be growing upon her; and since her return from the West she displayed more respect and affection for him than ever before.

A day or two after this conversation, Mr. Norris was attacked by a serious illness, and for a day or two his life was despaired of. Mrs. Plyne wrote to her brother, telling him of his father's dangerous condition, and begging him to come to them without delay. But the violence of the attack subsided upon the morning of the third day, and the physician pronounced his patient likely to recover. Good nursing and constant care were not wanting. Mrs. Plyne was an expert in that most trying and tiresome occupation, taking care of the sick, and Annie felt anxious and remorseful, thinking perhaps that solicitude for her, and the disappointment of his darling scheme, might have been the primary cause of his illness; so she devoted herself to his care until he was on the way to recovery.

One evening, Annie, after remaining nearly all the afternoon with Mr. Norris, waiting upon and nursing him, went out into the garden to rest, and think, and breathe the fresh air. She took the garden scissors with her, and gathered a bouquet of early flowers and green sprigs, which she intended for the invalid's room. As she re-entered the house, she heard the bustle of an arrival in the hall, and Mrs. Plyne's voice exclaiming, "My dear brother! Yes, he is much better. Come into the parlor."

Annie escaped, without being observed, to her own room; she began to dread the approaching *denouement,* and as she sat by the open window of her chamber, toying with her flowers, the color came and went upon her cheek; she blushed, and smiled, and paled alternately, pulling her flowers to pieces in a very nervous and fidgety manner meanwhile.

In about half an hour the tea-bell rang, and Mrs. Plyne came bustling to the door, and with only the pretense of a knock, entered.

"Brother has come, Annie. He is waiting in father's room to be introduced to you before going down to tea. Father seems almost well again this evening!"

Annie arose and followed Mrs. Plyne to her father's room. Standing, with one hand resting upon the back of the large easy-chair in which the invalid reclined, was a manly and well-known figure.

"Miss Howard, my brother Charles," began Mrs. Plyne, but "brother Charles," without waiting for further ceremony, sprung forward with an exclamation of pleasure and surprise, seized two little hands, and pressed them within his own, while a pair of ruby lips were offered for a kiss, and two amazed and bewildered people looked on in utter astonishment.

"How came you here, Annie? And you never wrote me of your intentions. I mailed a letter to *you,* after I left Thurston, on my way here." Just then the "Miss Howard" of his sister's introduction flashed across his remembrance, and an expression of perplexity took possession of his countenance. Annie burst forth into a musical peal of laughter.

"Do you think, 'Mr. Clark,' that no one can masquerade but yourself?"

Tea was neglected, and a full explanation entered upon; but the cook, who had taken extra pains to have a nice supper in honor of the guest, declared to Patty, the chambermaid, that she "Wasn't a-goin' to hab eberyt'ing jes' done spiled!" and accordingly, after ringing the bell twice without effect, made her appearance at the open door of the chamber and announced *supper* in her superbest style, and Mrs. Plyne declared that explanations and narratives must be postponed until the meal was over. The little party, however, were too much excited to have much appetite for Minty's good things, and that personage was extremely indignant at the indifference with which her dainties were treated.

They were all soon reassembled in the invalid's room, and the conversation resumed. Mr. Norris, with an attempt at humor quite unusual with him, declared that he had "made the match," after all.

"If I had not attempted to 'manage' Annie as I did, she would not have gone West, and Charlie would not have met, wooed and won her, for, of course, even if I had succeeded in bringing you together here, you would not have treated each other with common civility, so I shall no longer reproach myself, as I have done, for driving my little girl away from home, but console myself with the thought that, 'All's well that ends well!'"

Clark, as Annie still called him, made a much longer and more pleasant visit than he anticipated. His father rapidly recovered health and spirits. Mrs. Plyne confided to him that an eligible widower had proposed to make her Mrs. Clinton; and that, as soon as Annie was married, so that she would not be required to matronize the home-establishment, she should accept the proposition.

One of the first excursions which the young people took was out to Mr. Malor's farm, and Susie was confidentially invited to spend a month in town with her friend, that said friend might have the benefit of her advice and assistance in preparing for a certain important event which was to transpire in October—Annie's favorite month.

It seemed desirable that Annie's husband, when she took one, should be a resident of L——, as there were important interests there to be attended to in her behalf; and so "Clark" was persuaded, after much argument pro and con, to close his business connections in Thurston, and come to Annie's home, instead of taking her, as he wished to do, to one of his own—a proper penalty for marrying an heiress!

Of course there was a grand wedding in October. Poke and his wife, Melissy, were pressed into the service in the culinary and preparatory departments down-stairs, and many were the exclamations of astonishment and wonder elicited by him, when relating the remarkable occurrences of "out West."

THE END.

SUGGESTED READING

American Women's Dime Novel Project, George Mason University, http://chnm.gmu.edu/dimenovels/.

Cox, Randolf. *The Dime Novel Companion*. Greenwood Press, Westport, Conn., 2000.

Johannsen, Albert. *The House of Beadle and Adams and Its Nickel and Dime Novels; The Story of a Vanished Literature*. The University of Oklahoma Press, Norman, Okla., 1950.

——. *The House of Beadle and Adams and Its Nickel and Dime Novels; The Story of a Vanished Literature,* supplement edition. The University of Oklahoma Press, Norman, Okla., 1962.

Sullivan, Larry E., and Lydia Shuman. *Pioneers, Passionate Ladies, and Private Eyes: Dime Novels, Series Books & Paperbacks.* Haworth Press, Binghamton, N.Y., 1996.